The New Orleans of Possibilities

OTHER FICTION BY DAVID MADDEN

Novels
The Beautiful Greed (1961)
Cassandra Singing (1969)
Brothers in Confidence (1972)
Bijou (1974)
The Suicide's Wife (1978)
Pleasure-Dome (1979)
On The Big Wind (1980)

Collected Short Stories
The Shadow Knows (1970)

The New Orleans of Possibilities

STORIES BY DAVID MADDEN

Louisiana State University Press
Baton Rouge and London   1982

Copyright © 1982 by David Madden
All rights reserved
Manufactured in the United States of America
Design: Joanna Hill
Typeface: Garamond #3
Composition: G&S Typesetters, Inc.
Printing: Thomson-Shore
Binding: John Dekker & Sons

The author gratefully acknowledges permission to reprint some of these stories in this volume
from *December*, *Twigs*, *Southern Review*, *Minnesota Review*, and *North American Review*. "The
Cartridge Belt" is reprinted by permission of *Massachusetts Review* © 1972, The Massachusetts
Review, Inc.

LIBRARY OF CONGRESS CATALOGING IN PUBLICATION DATA

Madden, David, 1933–
    The New Orleans of possibilities.

    Contents: A part in Pirandello—The fall of the house of Pearl—The New Orleans of
possibilities—[etc.]   I. Title.
PS3563.A339N4   813'.54   81-19370
ISBN 0-8071-1008-6   AACR2
ISBN 0-8071-1015-9 (pbk.)

FOR MY MOTHER AND FOR MY BROTHER JOHN

Contents

The New Orleans of Possibilities

A Part in Pirandello

"Well, Mr. Cameron, as of now," said Mr. McMillan, letting the research paper slip from his hand, flop on the desk, "you've earned a D-minus in the course."

As Brent stared at "Extinct Volcanoes in the Orient" A-plus, his stomach felt as it did the time he rose against the wobbling of the vaulting pole and crashed his head backward against the cross-bar. Brent saw McMillan flinch at the expression on Brent's face.

"But, sir, that's what I had *before*. I thought this paper . . . ."

"I *know* you did." The office was so cramped their knees almost touched. "Compared with your earlier themes, this research paper shows a remarkable improvement in your ability to think, to organize your thoughts, and to express them." Looking narrow-eyed and quizzically into Brent's eyes, McMillan waited for him to respond.

Brent shrugged, closed his eyes. McMillan was a good teacher, a good man, but as he had said the first day of class, "When it comes to cheating, I'm a bastard." Brent *wanted* him to be a bastard, so he could confess, rid himself of the stranger in him who had turned to Kester for help. The doubts about Kester that had worried Brent even back in their early high school days in Ironton made this unconfessed crime twice repugnant. He wished he could vomit.

When he opened his eyes, he would confess and be free of what nagged him about Kester, too. They would kick him out of Melbourne, but kick him out clean, not secretly covered with slime. He never minded fumbling passes, placing third, missing baskets in *public*, because it was in public that he was always striving to make touchdowns, break finish tapes, make baskets, and sometimes did. But private, secret thorns festered.

Licking his lips, Brent opened his eyes. "Sir—"

"Mis—" McMillan stuck up a finger to stop him, "—ter Cameron, I *know* what this means to you. Loss of the sports scholarship, which means, for a young man from a steel town, being dropped from school—and into Vietnam. Going to be a dentist, weren't you?"

"Well, sir," said Brent, untangling his twisted fingers and spreading his hands apart, "the way things look *now* . . ."

"Something just occurred to me. You hear about the play I'm directing?"

"No, sir."

"Oh." A flicker of contempt. "Well, it's by Pirandello, *It Is So (If You Think So)*, sometimes translated *Right You Are, If You Think You Are*. Mysterious. Not a mystery—*psychologically* mysterious. Now, I've got some town ladies coming in to do the older women's parts, but I don't have a tall, beautiful girl to do Signora Ponza, wife of the new secretary of the provincial council. . . . She doesn't appear until the climax of the play, for about three minutes, and she's wearing a black veil over her face until her last line: 'No! I am she whom you believe me to be.' Now, you could memorize a few brief speeches like that, couldn't you?"

"Sir, I don't see . . ."

"Simple. I would feel justified in giving you credit in this course for work done in the play."

"You want me—to—dress up?"

"Crude way to put it, Mr. Cameron. This is not a fraternity romp. This is a serious, witty, play. One of my favorites, in fact. You would impersonate a young woman as convincingly as possible."

"*I* can't act, sir."

McMillan looked into his eyes. Brent tried not to blink. "Mr. Cameron, you are acting right at this moment."

"Sir—"

"Don't push it."

Brent *wanted* to push it—out. Out into the open. Be done with it. I'm guilty—on with the punishment. Though McMillan's reputation as a bastard about cheating had been justified in every instance, he treated each case individually and always put the culprit through the kind of hell he brought on himself. The student who tried to bluff all the way went out on his ear. If he confessed, he failed the course instantly, but was often persuaded to venture upon creative, sometimes profound alternatives for atoning with himself for his crime. Some of these students achieved great things during their chosen method of atonement, and ended up loving McMillan. Brent felt his own spirit go out to such possibilities. But *this* proposal did not at all resemble the kind of intricate moral situations Brent had heard tales of.

"You're worried about the other boys, right? Well, don't. I'll announce that a mystery woman, an old actress friend of mine, is coming to play the part."

"But, sir, the guys'll find out somehow."

Brent saw in his eyes that McMillan was still a step ahead of him. Brent wished he could get on his feet, move around. On a basketball court instead of this tiny closed room where they consciously had to avoid each other's knees, his mind might outmaneuver McMillan's.

"We'll have closed rehearsals, about midnight, just for your part. *I* don't want anybody to know. So together we'll keep this concealed until the moment you step out onto that stage."

"—and fall flat on my face."

"*I'll* be damned. Look, I haven't watched you on the basketball court, but I see you in the halls and on campus, walking. You don't even *sit* like the others. There's a *something* that I *know* I can get in shape, and it'll knock them out of their seats. You know, in the Greek theater, boys always played the female roles. Your great, athletic Greeks. Some young hero at Marathon or Thermopylae could have played Electra the spring before in Athens. Use your imagination, Cameron. Move a while in another dimension of yourself. . . . As you seem to have done in the style of this research paper."

"They'll recognize my face."

"Makeup is a mask. And it won't be *you* behind the mask."

"You make it sound so easy."

"Then you're not listening to what I *don't* say. Learning to walk like a lady will be very difficult. But when you go on that stage, you'll be Signora Ponza."

"And there's no *girl* who's right for the part?"

"I've beaten the bushes from one end of the county to the other. I was just about to switch to another play, when, suddenly, there *you* were, with your extinct volcanoes, your D-minus, and your dilemma."

Coach MacFarland patted his buttocks as he passed, and Brent felt light as a crane, listening to the ball he had hookshot into the basket bounce behind him as he ran out to receive again.

"What are *you* doing here?"

Kester stood between the collapsible bleachers back under the exit sign, holding his books against his chest, watching.

"Just wondering how you made out, Old Sport."

"McMillan gave me A-plus on the damned paper."

"Watch it!"

The blow against the side of his head made Brent go black a moment, then he chased the bouncing ball, blinking into clear vision as it rolled back toward him from the wall by the water fountain.

Brent had never entered Memorial Theatre through the *front* door, much less the back. He had missed, with little regret, two plays, one of them a required Shakespeare. Five minutes early, keeping in the shadows of the shrubs and trees close to the wall, Brent circled the building, unable to discover even a faint night light. No moon, no stars, pitch black, the bite of November in the air.

The stage door slipped open so easily he almost flung it into his own face. A light on an iron stanchion lit the stage. Used to a gleaming court, a well-lighted hive of faces, colorfully clothed bodies suddenly jumping to their feet, Brent stepped into the glare, feeling black-purple velvet hanging around him. He squinted at the darkness beyond the stage, suddenly imagining the audience that, two weeks from Friday, would fill the theater.

"Jesus, Mr. Cameron, you scared the hell out of me!"

"Sorry, sir, I just thought I'd better slip in."

"I'm over *here*. By the exit light."

"What do I do now, sir?"

"Take off your windbreaker."

Though it seemed he had spent most of his life undressing in front of men, Brent felt as if he were stripping nude before the whole school. Affecting nonchalance, he let the jacket dangle by his thumb over his shoulder.

"Now, walk upstage." Brent walked up to the dark footlights. "I'm sorry. *Up*stage means toward the rear." Brent's tennis shoes bumped together, squeaked, as he turned. "And spread the curtains a little to improvise an entrance." Smothery darkness between the velvet curtain and the wall he sensed but could not see. Heavy velvet muffled McMillan's voice: "Now, step out and walk very slowly, but in your natural gait, toward the footlights, *down*stage." Trying to imitate a girl, Brent waddled to the center of the stage before McMillan stopped him. "Mr. Cameron, toss the jacket aside. Now, listen, carefully. Walk *naturally*." Brent remembered that McMillan had said "your natural gait." "We've got plenty of time."

"Sorry, sir." Brent went behind the curtains again.

"I had the boys strip the stage. I want us to start from nothing and gradually work up to Signora Ponza's entrance opening night."

"Mac, does he have to be here?"

"Who?"

"Kester Dunlap."

Coach MacFarland looked around and stopped to get Kester, perched on the top bench of the collapsible bleachers, in focus. "Didn't even *see* him."

"You look around and suddenly he's there. Gives me the creeps."

"Well, you boys could do with an audience, couldn't you? Pre-game cheering section?"

"Practice ought to be closed to outsiders."

"Well, it ain't, Brent, so show him what you can do."

Brent made three baskets in a row, and on his way to the showers, some of the guys gave him a pat and his roommate gave him a quick hug as he passed.

"Again."

Anger almost suffocating him, Brent stood behind the dusty velvet curtain, waiting for McMillan to cue him.

"'*You must not irritate him. You must leave him alone. Oh, Please!*' . . . We're waiting, Mr. Cameron."

Brent walked out. Even with the rehearsal chairs, the stage felt empty, as though he slogged through a field of sludge.

Out there in the dark, McMillan beat on the back of a seat with a pencil. Brent wished he could see the man. He was never where the sound seemed to come from. Maybe it was part of his directing technique, like some of the tricks MacFarland used. The last tap of the pencil was like a pistol shot at the end of a quarter.

"Mr. Cameron."

"Sir?"

"I can't help but wonder whether you're trying to convince me that you're all wrong for this part."

"I'm trying to do what you tell me to, sir."

"Yes, Mr. Cameron, you *are* doing what I tell you to. But that's *all* you're doing."

"I don't know what else to *do*."

"Have you read the play yet?"

"No, sir, I had to study for a psych test."

"Read it. This weekend. Think about it. And I'll see you Monday."

Brent slept through most of the weekend. He would master himself enough to open the book, then fall asleep after every five pages. During long lapses into stupor, he stared at the black, purple, green, and white cover: *Naked Masks/ Five Plays/ By Luigi Pirandello*.

Brent wished his roommate had not gone away to visit his girl. With his roommate's Hendrix record going, Brent would have had an excuse for not concentrating. No parties at Melbourne that weekend either. No games. Only Pirandello and assignments in four courses, including McMillan's English class. An interpretation of "The Force That Through the Green Fuse Drives the Flower"— whatever the hell that meant. Dylan Thomas' phrases made Brent's head feel as though his body were adrift in a tiny boat.

He wrote to his mother, but didn't feel at all like writing to his father.

So far Brent had only practiced walking, hardly listening to McMillan reel off the lines. At three AM, Monday morning, he finally read up to the scene he had dreaded: "*Signora Ponza* (turning her veiled head with a certain austere solemnity toward her husband): Don't be afraid!" Suddenly, the fact that he would have to speak like a woman struck him. The sound of his voice as he tried to speak her next speech nauseated him: "*Signora Ponza* (having looked at them through her veil, speaking with dark solemnity): What else do you want of me, after this, ladies and gentlemen? There is a misfortune here, as you see, which must stay hidden; otherwise the remedy which our compassion has found cannot avail." But as he read the rest of her six brief speeches, Brent felt more composed.

"You have to admit," he said, to his face in the mirror over the washroom sink, "It's kinda interesting."

At breakfast, he sat with the boys on the team, laughing so hard at their dirty jokes that he cried, almost hysterically. Seeing the tears, they pointed at him and pretended to jeer as he wiped them away. A hive of nerves, knowing he must sit still and collect himself, he let the boys drift off in groups, until he was alone at the messy table.

"I got an A in Seventeenth Century."

Brent's flesh jumped. He turned toward the table behind, and Kester's face, twisted around on the stalk of his neck, was only a foot away.

"Great." Kester had tested out of freshman English.

"You'd probably get an A, too, if you were in there with *me*."

"I'd regret it, too."

"Don't *be* that way, Brent, hell, we're from the same home town."

"That's an accident."

"True, we didn't choose to be born in Ironton, but that we went to kindergarten, grammar school, junior high, high school, and now to one of the best men's colleges in the country together can't be ruled out as superfluous."

"Stop pretending you like sports so much! And stop coming to rehearsals like that."

"Rehearsals?"

"I mean practice—basketball."

"Moral support, Old Sport. You didn't make those three baskets in a row like that till I waved to you."

McMillan seemed so pleased when he thought up the idea of having Brent wear basketball shorts and go barefoot that Brent hadn't the heart to tell him how *he* felt about it. Walking out onto the stage barefoot, in shorts, was a shock. But McMillan knew what he was doing.

Even "out in life," McMillan had a reputation for doing everything in a slightly theatrical manner, though most of the time you didn't even *know* it until you had *enjoyed* it. But *no*body could enjoy *this*. Still, Brent had to admit that the idea of starting from nothing, from scratch, made sense.

"'No, no, madam, for yourself you must be either one or the other!'"

"'*No! I am she whom you believe me to be.*'" Through an imaginary thick black veil, Brent looked at all the imaginary people.

"'*Laudisi*: And there, my friends, you have the truth! Are you satisfied?'" McMillan enacted Laudisi's derisive laugh. "Curtain! It's getting better, Mr. Cameron. Once more."

Brent did a smart about-face and started upstage. The door frame made it seem more real. He was eager to do it with walls on each side.

He wouldn't be surprised if McMillan asked him to come out next wearing only his jock.

*   *   *

"I was talking to some townie in this bar—says Stella screws anything that moves. Legend in her own times." Naked, Brent's roommate rattled his locker door.

Brent laughed so hard he cried, and his teammates laughed at him, and the laughter and gentle shoving eased him like watching rainbow trout in a mountain stream.

"How 'bout *you*, Brent? You like to take a turn?"

"Sure. Love to."

"Ever love it *before*?"

"Sure."

"Ah, come on, Brent. Admit it. You're a virgin, right?"

"Well . . ."

"Wasn't you the big football hero at Ironton?"

"Well . . ."

"Sure, he was. My old man used to take the Ironton *Courier*, and we kept track of him."

"Well, there was plenty of girls, you know, but I only had *one*."

"*Had* her?"

"No, I mean *sweet*heart."

"How come she never comes up?"

"She's still in high school."

"Robbin' the cradle, Brent?"

"Well . . ."

"How 'bout Stella? You can *have* some, if you crave it."

"Sure, I'll go along."

"Hell. Even ol' McMillan knocks it off."

"Who says?"

"This townie I was talking to. Stella loves to brag. You know, big English professor."

"Talks like a queer in class." The imitation of a "queer" was perfect.

"He don't talk like a queer, man."

"You're not even in McMillan's class, man!"

"All that poetry!"

"Jesus! The man's a stud. Used to make it with his students at that university. Kicked him out for it."

"Look, don't jump on *me*."

"*Jump* on you? I'll stomp hell out of you. McMillan's cool."

"You ever see him at sports events?"

"I don't *look* for him. I'm playing *ball*, man."

"This guy said Stella told him McMillan begged her to be in this play he's getting up."

"Hey, wouldn't *that* be groovy!" He popped a locker door with his towel. "All us guys out there that's cut her. What an uprising!"

Voices from both sides of the row of lockers volleyed toward Brent.

"Why did she back out?" Brent's face was burning.

"See, this townie's a special friend of hers, don't even make it with her, and she told him she wanted to keep it a secret from *each* of us that she's going with *all* of us. And mainly, she's afraid if we all sit out there and see her, we'll start cheering and stomping, and mainly McMillan'll find out he ain't the only one. Says McMillan's got this purity complex about women, and he's convinced himself Stella's clean."

"What a mind that girl's got. And dropped out in the tenth!"

"Hey, guys, let's make Brent laugh till he cries. I love to watch him."

Brent walked toward the footlights, aware that the stage, midnight, the dark, the presence in the auditorium affected his own walk even before rehearsal began. "Sir?" he said to the dark.

"Good evening, Mr. Cameron." McMillan sounded very tired. "Tonight, I want you to come out nude."

"Sir . . ."

"Yes?" He sounded like a doctor telling Brent to cough. Brent gave up, feeling that to *talk* about it would only make it worse. Because he knew he would *do* it.

Undressing behind the curtain, dropping his clothes over a music stand, it occurred to him that if Stella had not refused the part, he wouldn't *be* here. He had avoided meeting her, going to bed with her, and the boys hadn't pushed it, as though they respected his virginity, realized it was reserved for the "right girl," and he was grateful.

"Mr. Cameron."

"Yes, sir."

"Do you think you can find your way in the dark?"

"I think so."

"Then I'm going to turn out the work light, and I want you, at your *own* speed and in your own mood, while trying to retain the *feeling* of Signora Ponza, to make your entrance, do the movements I've blocked, and deliver your lines in total darkness. Do you know *why* I'm doing this?"

Without stopping to think, Brent said, "Yes, sir, I understand."

After rehearsal, Brent slipped into the dark gym and groped among the basketballs and went out onto the court and dribbled from one end to the other. He aimed at a gleam of light on the rim of a basket. The sound of the ball bouncing off the board sickened him. It rolled under the bleachers, and he had to crawl in the dark.

Gradually he stripped off all his clothes, even his tennis shoes. And after a long while, drenched with sweat in the cold building where the heat had been turned off for the night, he began to make baskets.

The shoosh through the net lifted his pulse and he floated in the dark, imagining himself as Mercury, then feeling like Mercury, and for an instant, as he tossed the last ball, he *was* Mercury.

Late Thursday afternoon, Brent happened to pass through Herald Hall, short-cutting through the quadrangle, late for basketball practice, when he saw Kester sitting in McMillan's office, his books perched on his touching knees, McMillan sitting sideways rared back in his swivel chair, his feet propped up on his desk, an awkward posture of avoidance. Seeing Brent stride past, Kester flicked his hand up, and McMillan turned his head toward the door. But Brent missed his expression.

Brent ran through crisp leaves that lay thick under the close-standing maples, stirring up waves of sound that carried him to the gym door where sunlight glared on the panes.

Kester didn't come to watch practice. When Brent realized that he had made no baskets, he tried harder, then very hard.

Above the roar of the ten showers, somebody down by the door yelled: "What was the matter with you today, Brent?"

"Oh, I was just thinking of Stella."

They all laughed, jumping up and down, feet splashing, bodies glistening.

That night, Brent stripped before he even presented himself on stage. Not until he walked through the wide parlor entrance into the full glare of footlights—turned on for the first time, revealing ornate, heavy Victorian furniture and mock mirrors and Rococo clocks—did he imagine the surprise McMillan would feel at suddenly seeing him there, naked on stage.

"Sir?"

High heeled silver slippers set side by side, glittering in the footlights.

"Sir?"

He had come to feel McMillan's presence out there in the darkness as vividly as when their knees almost touched during conferences in his office. McMillan was not out there. The silence told Brent what was expected of him.

He bent over, picked up the shoes. Then he put them back, stood straight. He knelt, as a young lady would, to pick them up again, then went back through the door, closed it, and stepped into the slippers in the dark, wondering whether McMillan was only pretending not to be out there.

"Wasn't Brent great tonight?" asked Kester, coming up to McMillan and three other students at the Deke victory party. Brent overheard, standing with another group by the window.

"I didn't see the game. I detest sports. Except for the solitary ones—running, pole vaulting, the man against himself, triumphing over himself."

"Well, sir, you don't know what you're missing. Brent finally broke through tonight. Everybody at home always felt he was holding back. Something's brought it out."

"Excuse me," McMillan said to the three students, "I must circulate, like a good chaperon."

"He's a bastard."

"Watch your mouth, Kester," said Brent, coming over to him, as the three students ambled away.

"What cause have *you* to stick up for him, Old Sport?"

"You always drink more than you can hold, Kester."

"Something bothering me, Old Sport."

Brent didn't want to know *what*.

"Don't you walk away from me. We used to play together when we were little."

"Nobody wants to hurt your feelings, Kester." Brent hoped that pacified him.

"Think nothing of it." Kester looked up at the ceiling. "I love it, obviously."

By the phonograph, shuffling through the records, aware that his roommate's girl was staring soulfully at him, Brent glanced over at Kester. He was still staring up at the ceiling. Brent looked up.

Brent swung his body among the desks from the back row toward the classroom door, watching the last student go out.

McMillan, gathering his usual load of books, looked up. "Want to see me?"

"Kester Dunlap . . ."

"Oh, God."

"We better watch out for him."

"We'd better what?"

"He's sneaky."

"Yes, I know he's sneaky."

"He was the one helped me write that—"

"That's past. And your work is improving, by the way."

"I'm failing Psych 7."

"I ought to kick your tail, Mr. Cameron."

"I'm sorry, sir, I try. But I've got basketball and—no, forget that, sir. I don't want to whine."

"Good. Now, what about Kester Dunlap *otherwise?*"

"I don't know, sir. I was just saying we got to watch him."

Frowning, McMillan looked so straight into his eyes that Brent blinked.

"Dress rehearsal tomorrow night, Mr. Cameron."

"With the others, sir?"

"No. They won't see you until you make your entrance opening night. I want to give *them* the same impact I give the audience, even at the risk of throwing them."

"Makeup tomorrow night?"

"Yes, and full costume. You're handling the costume very well."

"You going to help me put the makeup on? I don't know the first thing about it."

"Try it yourself first. Then we'll see. Work at it until you make yourself look like what you know the boys will want to see in a beautiful face. Pirandello doesn't let her lift the veil, but just for that last line, '*No! I am she whom you believe me to be,*' I want them to see her face for a moment."

"Will I be able to see them when I lift the veil?"

"Can you see *me?*"

"No, sir."

"Cameron."

"Yes, sir?"

Usually, McMillan gave commands like Major Scott in ROTC, but sometimes he spoke softly, as he did about poetry in class, and Brent had to strain to hear him out there in that theatrical darkness.

"How do you feel?"

"Fine."

"Awkward?"

"No, sir."

"Embarrassed?"

"No, sir."

"Exactly how *did* you feel a moment ago?"

"I can't say."

"Yes, you can."

"Like I was Stella."

"Who?"

"Signora Ponza!" Quickly, to cover, he asked, "Well, sir, how did it look to *you*?"

"Perfect."

MacFarland gave Brent a harder slap than usual. "Murder 'em, kid!"

The curtain was going up. After the game, he would just have time to dash to the theater for the climax.

By half time, Brent had done nothing but stumble.

"Brent?"

"Yes, sir."

"What happened to the grace?"

"The what?"

"The grace you used to have? One thing you always had out there worth watching was grace. Only word for it. Decoration, maybe. Least you could decorate the play with grace, even when you didn't make it on the baskets. Now, I can't even *look* at you."

When Brent went back onto the gleaming court, he tried to move with grace. Bumped off balance once, he landed square. His feet cocked up, he slid four feet and slammed into the wall by the water fountain.

MacFarland didn't put his head in his hands this time. He just stared at Brent, mouth open.

At the end of the game, Brent saw Kester leave with the crowd, and his heart was light, knowing that Kester wouldn't be in the audience when he walked out onto the stage fifteen minutes from now.

The shock of cold water was greater than Brent had ever felt. He worked the water up to as hot as he could stand it, enveloping himself in steam, standing in the middle of the shower room, his eyes closed. He wished the end nozzle in the corner were not in use. The shouts of victorious players in the other dressing room penetrated

the cinder block walls. Brent's teammates were silent, each feeling
responsible, but he sensed that they blamed him most. Though he
was seldom great, he had never been bad. Never, as MacFarland put
it, graceless.

With one of the keys McMillan had secured for him, Brent entered the theater through the boiler room door. In a corner, under
the air ducts, sat a dressing table, lit up, and from a steam pipe
hung the black dress, the hat, the veil. The slippers—black ones,
not the silver rehearsal shoes—were on the table beside the makeup.

The secrecy of the setup aggravated his nervousness. But he was
not too nervous to observe—as he rose and stepped backward toward
the hum of the furnace to look at himself—that the face in the mirror was, indeed, as McMillan had said, "perfect." Perhaps the word
was *beautiful*.

He let fall the veil and inserted the brass key. *The door to the regular dressing room also will be locked. Only you can open it.* He opened the
door, stepped into the deserted dressing room, and crossed it, shivering. But as he climbed the stairs, he realized that what he was
feeling was not nervousness—it was thrill.

People were working backstage. *Don't let them throw you. It will at
first, maybe, because you aren't used to seeing them there, but you must stay
absolutely in character.* They turned in the faint light to stare, trying
to play it cool. But Brent knew that the suspense and mystery made
them aware of the beating of their own hearts as he was aware of his
own. *Will she reveal herself at the curtain call? they are wondering.*

*When you exit, go straight back the way you came—don't run—stay in
character, even in front of the backstage crew, as you leave. Lock the doors
behind you.* Brent stood behind the masking, waiting for his cue, trying to shut out MacFarland's voice and eyes: *What happened to the
grace?*

A voice behind him said, "I'm your husband, Miss."

Brent turned, even more startled to see the face—heavily lined
with mascara and rouge, the mouth defined by a false mustache—of
the boy who sat next to him in psych class, who passed every test

with an A-plus. The boy himself was taking a deep breath, looking
at a strange girl—overwhelmed.

"*'You must not irritate him. You must leave him alone. Oh, please!'*"
Not McMillan's voice cueing him this time, but the strange voice of
a woman.

"Well, you're *on*." When the boy touched his arm, Brent felt and
saw a spark.

He stepped out into the entrance of the parlor in Italy.

"Who is it?"

"Kester."

"Go away. I'm asleep."

"You better stop acting so hateful."

"Who *is* that out there?" Brent's roommate looked out from under his pillow.

"Kester Dunlap."

"Hey, boy, you better get away from that door, 'fore I come out
there and chew your arm right off your shoulder."

Afraid somebody would recognize him, Brent did not show up at
the dining room Saturday morning. For the first time, he missed
breakfast with the team. But he couldn't sleep. He lay on his cot and
tried to feel real.

The door shot open, straight-armed, and Brent's roommate and
three other jocks came in.

"Looks like I'm going to be a playgoer!"

"Hell, me, too!"

"Why didn't somebody *tell* us?"

"Hell, we was bouncing balls all over the place, man, while *she*—"

"Jesus, I never saw guys so excited."

"I was so certain she'd turn out to be Stella after all, I didn't feel
too bad about not being there opening night—figured I might go to
one of the other performances."

"Hey, Brent, you awake or asleep?"

Brent kept still, made no sound.

*   *   *

At lunch, Brent listened to the talk himself.

He ate a light supper at the Dutchman's, the only other eating place in Melbourne.

He walked in the woods until time to perform.

Sunday morning, he went to breakfast. By now, everyone had seen the mysterious lady.

"Hell, I'm going again tonight."

"Most beautiful woman I ever laid eyes on."

"*Girl* is more like it."

"I'd give my left—"

"Ah, watch it, man, she's a damn nice girl."

"How *you* know?"

"Can't you tell by looking at her?"

"Hell, they all the same. They all *like* it."

"All, huh? How *you* know?"

"Ones I ain't had, I ain't met."

"Bull."

"Well, *he'll* bull you, boys, but if you want to know what it's like, *I* can tell you. 'Cause last night after the show, she was hotter'n hell, full of the feeling the guys gave her, sitting out there burning like wicks, so I *got* me some."

"What was it like?"

"Hell, I'm sorry, she swore me to secrecy."

They all laughed until they nearly cried. Brent's laughter, sounding as false as a cracked bell, made them look at him.

In the dressing room, he tried to keep away from the others, but they ambled up to him quite naturally, as though his body, like their own, were a low-powered magnet. Unbuttoning his shirt, he felt the starch brush against his nipples.

"Love to seen her in a tighter dress, wouldn't you?"

"Yeah, it hung too loose."

"I ain't swimming in the same pool with *you* guys. I like my water *cold*."

"Just like to brush with my two thumbs the places where her mourning dress seemed to rise from the dead."

"Man, I'm suffering. Suffering."

"Know how you feel. Sticky dreams."

"McMillan cold-cocked Bronson with the poetry book 'cause he was putting a fourth act on that play, sitting there glassy-eyed. 'It's *your* fault, sir,' he said, and McMillan blushed, and said he was sorry, but we was all laughing. Ol' Bronson, too."

Brent stood with one trouser leg off, balanced on one foot, and slowly pulled the other off, feeling every inch of cloth against his skin.

"Thing about *her* is guys talk dirty 'bout wanting to lay her, you know, but you can tell by their voices they don't think it's right, yet they plow right on. You know?"

"Yeah."

"I'll be honest. I'd just like to *kiss* her one time."

Brent followed them toward the showers.

"Yeah, well, I know what you mean, but when you come right down to it, I'd love to stroke her from ear*lobe* to tip*toe*." The envisioned ecstasy made him let out a raucous scream that roared in the tiled shower room, and as he turned the shower full gush, he looked at Brent through the steam. "Wouldn't you, Brent?"

Awkwardly, standing on the raised sill of the shower room, Brent turned, slipped, staggered, and almost ran back to the locker, reaching for his clothes.

Brent lay on his cot through the supper hour. But avoiding the team only made the things they had said over the past three days come back more lucidly. He saw their faces, and the strange new ways they used their hands.

His flesh burned. When he felt his jock begin to fill and stretch, he jumped up and walked quickly out of the room and down the stairs.

*   *   *

"Yes?"

"You Stella?"

"Yeah."

"I wonder if you'd let me come in."

"What you so nervous about?" She had lowered her voice.

"Stage fright."

"Haven't I seen you some place before?"

"That's a good line," said Brent. "Can I come in?"

"I don't even *know* you." The room behind her was brightly lighted, full of cigar smoke.

"The guys said you were pretty friendly."

"Look, I don't just go out with anybody, anytime."

"Who is it, Stella, some salesman?" McMillan's voice, so casual, natural, startled Brent.

"Yeah, honey, I'm trying to get him to take no for an answer."

An indulgent chuckle—McMillan amused at an inept pun.

"We don't want none—*any*."

Brent turned away, nauseated.

"Hey!" she whispered.

"What?"

"*Now*, I remember. When you lifted that veil . . ." At the look in her eyes, Brent shivered. "They sent you to make fun of me, huh? Like the other one—the little one."

"Little one *who*?"

"Called him Keeser or Custer."

"That *you*, Old Sport?"

Up the main street of the toy town of Melbourne, Kester walked toward Brent along an iron fence.

"Keep walking, Kester—the other way."

"You better stop being so hateful to me."

"You needn't worry anymore."

"I've taken enough off you and him."

"You always *did* talk in tongues, Kester, like people in revival tents."

"I won't *tell*, Brent."

"What is there for you not to tell?"

Kester stood on the corner under the streetlight and looked at him. Brent stood in the dark on the sidewalk, afraid to get near Kester. "I saw you that first night, and I went back last night, and I'm going back again tonight. A lot of guys are going their third time. But I knew it was you the *first* night."

"You were at the basketball game the first night."

"I ran over for the ending."

"It's going to end without me tonight."

"Don't let the talk get you down."

"I'm hitting the road."

"You can't do McMillan that way. It's almost curtain time."

"So long, Kester."

"I promise I won't tell."

"Shut up, Kester."

"That's just how McMillan talked. I told him I wouldn't tell about you and him, and first he got mad, and then he laughed like I was an armless freak threatening to slap him, and it was like getting slapped myself, the way he laughed. He's the devil, Brent."

"Shut up, Kester."

"So when he was laughing at me, I decided there wasn't anything going on between you."

"Goddamn you, shut up!"

"Brent, it'll pass over. *I've* heard them talking, too. I walk around and *listen* to them. But they don't know, and I won't tell, and before long, after a few more games, you know, you'll forget it. *You can*, because there's nothing wrong with you, Brent." Brent glanced back. Kester was backing away, out of the streetlight. "Believe me, Brent." Kester backed into the dark under the thick new leaves of trees hanging over the street. "I promise not to come tonight. There's not a *thing* wrong with you!" Then Kester turned and walked through the main gates of the campus.

The leaves loud under his feet, Brent walked into the pool of light, a feeling of grace in his stride.

The Fall of the House of Pearl

Used cars are parked now where Pearl's house once stood. The lot lies just inside the city limits on the main highway. If it's night when you pass by, the colored lights, the wind-whipped banners and streamers, and the blinking neon signs make it a mock carnival. But with morning mist and no lights and the colors dull, you think of gray things, like the cars being full of wan shadows, the streamers—things left behind by a wanderlust idiot.

It was dawn when I passed in a Trailways bus coming in from San Francisco a few days ago. I've been gone two years. I strained my eyes against the wind-ripping speed of the bus, tense for a glimpse of Pearl's house. It was the kind of house that when you look at it you don't feel as though you're seeing anything. But if you look closer at its two stories, its warped, fan-shaped porch, its roof like dying moss, it's sort of an upright piano dipped in dirty whitewash, and the massive, sprawling sycamore is a buxom woman, hair flying, playing a raucous ditty. The house always seemed swollen with a sombre anticipation.

One hot day about three years ago when I was fifteen, I was riding home on a crowded bus. Steaming bodies in brief dresses and sweat-stuck shirts stood too close. Dull-eyed people hanging with a wilted, summer look from the hand-hooks made me think of cattle hanging by their hooves. Pearl was sitting up front, her thin arms crossed over the packages on her lap, going home after a day's work as a seamstress. I took out the snapshots I'd gotten from Walgreen's.

One of the shots was blank—an abortive attempt to photograph Pearl in her Sunday dress. The eighth picture was the result of one of

my odd moods. I took it standing outside Pearl's bedroom window
just at dusk. Grandma, Pearl's momma, was standing beside the
kitchen table loaded with steaming food, beneath that mammoth
light bulb that hung by its navel cord. She was wearing one of her
print dresses with microscopic daisies on it—and tennis shoes. She
had freckles on a rather stupid face, and she wore her dough-gray
hair in braids. So it was going to be a sensitive shot of an old woman
whose every thought springs from her function—daughter's slave
and son's eternal momma, a grandma without grandchildren. But
the result was a blur—an amoeba shape.

I leaned my cheek against the grille over the open window, trying
to suck a little air out of the furnace in the sky, but through all the
cattle I could see Pearl's old man, clutching his cane, standing behind the conductor, talking to him. That cane had enough TB
germs on it to murder an army. Pearl avoided riding the same streetcar as her father in the mornings. Only by accident were they there
so close. She looked through her father, as though he were steam,
sunsucked from the macadam.

The bus purred down the hill into the valley where we lived.

I got off at the back door, Pearl the front. The old man stood du-
biously beside the driver. He knew to go one more stop before getting off. Probably, Pearl had never said anything, but he knew. In
his own sick manner, he was diplomatic.

I watched her clip along the walk, puffing with the load of packages. Pearl was thirty-six, supposedly a virgin, and she was as tall as
her hair was long, which was slightly over six feet. It was black, and
she wore it like a helmet in braids roped tightly around her head.
Her face was sharp, slender, and maybe pretty. It had that per-
petually awed, astonished countenance peculiar to people of recent
mountain origin. Wide, bony hips gave her a lopsided appearance
like the tower of Pisa. She walked like a self-conscious goose.

I looked behind me, acting like someone had called my name, to
snatch a glimpse of the old man. The tall skinny form, hunched beneath a bag of rags, hobbled in a jolting gait. Twenty years ago on
the farm, he had broken his ankle and hadn't worked since. Now
and then he sold cleaning rags to filling stations. He was a drunk to

boot. His son, Thad, who had been born a cripple and a dwarf, worked like a mule. But lately Thad's eyes had been going out. My mother often said he was the only one of them worth a belch in hell.

From the way the old man ripped and raked his throat and lungs with bursting wet coughing, they must have been like one of those used netted rags after use—threadbare, oily, and limp as a dishrag. He looked almost, but not quite, like the kind of old man people enjoy being tender and jovial with. But when he hacked out in a sudden rage of coughing, you drew back and dodged, and the pity that tried to come out in your heart couldn't quite make it.

Pearl slammed the screen door, jarring flies from tightbrained sleep. She always slammed doors and took footsteps to be heard, especially at raw 6 AM when she went into the mist to work. Mother wasn't home yet so I had the upstairs all to myself.

Just as I was lowering my sweaty, grimy body into the tub, the garbled voice of a sports announcer drilled up through the floor. Staring in fixed irritation at the blue wall of the bathroom, I could picture the old man with his face up to the radio, his mouth hanging open, drooling, completely absorbed in what the man with the god-like voice was saying about the balls and bats. As usual, Pearl allowed his immersion in the only thing in life that still interested him to reach a trancelike state before she issued her queen-bee order of the day, and that was the end of that.

Standing in the cold water, I looked blandly down into the backyard, soaping between my legs. Grandma was chopping stubborn wood, and like a snail she lugged deep buckets of coal to the cookstove. It was she who raked the lawn, cooked most of the meals, scrubbed the house, washed the smelly clothes, tended her meager flowers in the big rotten tubs by the rear wall of the house, and worried until wisps from her plaited hair hung like cobwebs on her brow if one of her small clan was not home precisely according to routine. In twenty years she had been to town twice and to the nearby drugstore maybe five times.

I ate sardines. Then I went down and sat in the front porch swing to expose myself to some of the evening's stingy breeze. A lonely kid rode his bicycle up and down the sidewalk, pinching a rubber horn that grunted a nauseating sound. Hillbilly music blasted out from the four filling stations that spotted like greasy globs each corner of the block. Dogs ran barking in packs.

And the downstairs walls of the house trembled against the habitual balderdash of domestic squabbling, the malicious, teasing, insinuating words falling like gnats and wasps upon four passive brains.

Pearl was unfailingly the instigator. Like a sentry wrapped in the flag of his nation, she was ever on guard against a sign of hostility upon which she could pounce. When the rare silence got terrifying, she began to imagine the enemy lurking, tense for the strike.

From where I sat in the swing, I could see through the living room window on into the kitchen. Pearl towered over her mother, lashing her scapegoat with abuse for not knowing who did what with the picture postcard Hank sent. Flecks of her spittle showered down upon the stubby old woman's flushed face. She merely stood there, whining, blinking her eyes, fingering her frayed apron.

Then the telephone rang. There was a brief lull among the others while Pearl talked. She announced that it was Hank, and when she was finished, the voices in the room steadily rose to a quaking crescendo. Hank was a professional soldier and, at least by mail, he and Pearl had courted for seven years.

Thad emerged from the tavern across the street, dragging behind him his lame leg that scraped the pavement as he weaved among the huge trucks that roared like dinosaurs along the highway.

One leg was longer than the other but he didn't wear a raised shoe. He had long, powerful hairy arms. His hair was a black flowing mane. Blind in one eye, he was tortured by constant headaches from a cataract in the other. Standing four feet ten, he looked like a sort of cornpone Toulouse-Lautrec.

His mother had carried him on her hip until he was eight years old, and until he reached that suspicious age, he had slept with big sister Pearl. He held a part-time job in a radio shop, and all his money, except for the upkeep of his T-model Ford, went into the common treasury, over which glowered Pearl's vigilant eye.

Pearl met him on the porch and began a long, repetitious, emotional scrawl to the effect that Hank had just called long distance from where he was stationed in Baltimore. Thad's attitude was silently, infuriatingly indifferent. Pearl's elation drooped into whining resentment as she followed her brother into the house.

Sitting in the swing, watching the twilight thicken, feeling my own stomach's emptiness, I heard them eating, talking about "the call" in the brightly lit kitchen.

They devoured their food with gusto. Pearl was an excellent and extravagant cook, and they always sat down with their knees under enough food to feed a regiment. Because of his fits of coughing, the old man was, by order of Pearl, exiled to the kitchen where he ate his meals on a crate.

After each meal, when the broken music of silver and glass had ceased, and they were anchored upon their chairs, a loud, throaty belch unfailingly rent the air—Thad the dwarf, making his private noise in the world.

Thad's favorite evening pastime was tickling his mother, limp as a willow-whip after the long day's toil and Pearl's abuse. I would be reading, writing stories or staring out the window, when suddenly the house would catch its breath as the long spiel of insane laughter began. I never saw this exhibition, but I imagined her galloping screaming through the house, jarring the glass animals on the knick-knack rack, her fat hips scraping the door frames, the red-faced dwarf hobbling after her, dragging his bum foot, his hairy hands clawing the air. He would pin her to the floor or in a corner and her hips would grind the wood or the rose-papered wall as she writhed in a delirium of airy giggles.

They were in high gear when Pearl, preceded by the yawning of the screen door, came out onto the porch. All the porches in the block were loaded with stuffed, low-voiced shadows. Lightning bugs laced the dark. Rhapsodizing for nearly an hour over Hank the incomparable, she laid her fluttering heart in my lap.

Finally, she got up and strolled next door to the filling station, where Buster was leaning against a gas pump, peeling an apple. Though she was made for Hank in some heavenly conspiracy, she could be seen every evening standing, leaning left, her arms crossed over her little girl's breasts, chattering like an orangutang with silent Buster. Unknown to her, he called her Minnie Pearl to emphasize the comic, rural element in her pseudoproud mannerisms. When a cloud of gnats got in her hair, she went on to her next victim, the drugstore soda jerk.

Having made the exterior rounds, she returned to the living room powwow, where the event was bled dry, embalmed, and laid in state. It was finally cremated in the inferno of Pearl's nocturnal dreams.

Mother came home and we had supper.

I was sitting on the porch again, smoking a cigarillo, when I saw Emmett standing on the sidewalk. He always wore the same overalls and a green beanie, and wherever he went he pushed a rubber tire before him. He laid his tire on the curb and came quietly up on to the porch.

He was allowed to roam the city, and especially in the neighborhood he was well known and eventually came to be tolerated. It was perfectly natural for him to stroll through an open doorway anywhere.

He had the reputation of plaguing one family at a time. When he happened to begin his vigilance over the house of Pearl, it was the dead of winter. He would come into the house and stare at them. After awhile, they realized that it was no use throwing verbal abuse at him, flinging and batting their arms in unwelcome gestures, so they would merely sit there, uncomfortably pretending ignorance of his thick presence.

He always terrified me, so I sat stone-still, wordless, while he looked through the screen into the murky hall and then went to the light-struck window and stared in.

Grandma was reading a romance magazine, the likes of which she and Pearl devoured with gargantuan zeal. Thad was reading *Popular Mechanics*. Pearl was knitting a sweater for Hank. Her self-control finally shattered and she angrily drew the shade. Emmett's shadow was imprinted upon the shade by the streetlight. Suddenly, the house light blinked out.

I imagined her being nervously aware of him, though she no

longer saw any trace. She rose from the deep, soft chair, the sweater, suggested by some Arctic battle-front, in her hand, stealthily tip-toed to the window and took hold of the shade. It flipped from her clammy fingers and zoomed to the top, flapping like the wings of a giant bird. Then she saw Emmett still standing there staring into her eyes. Emmett disappeared through sedge brush, rolling his tire, leaving a whisper in the grass.

That night I lay awake, zipped up in a jacket of sweat, humidity, and mental stupor, while up from the filling station shot like sharp silver needles the relentless ticking of the air pump meter: ding-gock, ding-gock. I thought of Pearl lying in bed beside her soundly sleeping mother, she too tossing with each startling tick of the pump, as she bored the sandman with her gossip and her illusions of romantic grandeur married to Hank.

The air pump bell became too much to bear this side of insanity, so I went downstairs, wearing only my jock shorts. I stuffed paper in its mouth and ran through the grass back to the hallway.

The door to their apartment was open. A sudden explosion of light in the kitchen exposed Pearl's tall frame in purple silhouette as she stalked to the door inside her mauve nightgown that clung to her bones like mummy gauze. I tried not to look at her, made nude by the brightness, because I disliked her and resented the galloping of my pulse.

No doubt she was aware of the light. I imagined her in the sun-dead kitchen, sitting in her birthday suit on a white straight chair, her black hair a tent around her white body, washing her long, blue-veined feet with long, pale fingers, knowing very well that the married man next door was trying to read his evening paper by his own window.

"I fixed it for a while," I said, "but I guess it'll go on forever, one way or another," and returned to my sweat jacket.

A week later I was sitting by my window eating a peanut butter sandwich when I saw a soldier getting off the bus at the corner. He was coming along the walk when Emmett suddenly appeared and persuaded him to let him carry the duffel bag.

The fanfare upon his arrival was no more than a languid flurry of flesh and sound. The whine of the screen door as he entered, followed by grim Emmett, was preceded by a slamming door in the rear of the house—the old man imprisoned himself with the flies.

I expected Pearl to raise a ceremonial flag over the house. But she merely let him into it without a kiss or a promise—her heart, no doubt, a leaping frog in her throat. Grandma's smile adorned her awkwardness, Thad's iron handshake punctuated the occasion as his blind-struck eye leveled on nothing.

During the next few days there was a lot of sitting around in the dining room. Hank, a tall birchlike man with small brown hands, loose eyes, and limp hair, sitting with legs crossed precisely, looking meaningless and blank as far as I could see. Pearl baking fabulous pies and cakes, cooking massive meals, shutting herself against all the emotion that tried to puff out. Grandma still lugging coal and chopping wood. Thad reading *Popular Mechanics* as though oblivious to his coming blindness.

And the old man just lay on the narrow daybed I had loaned him, inhaling the damp darkness, staring up at the yellow ceiling, the room shuddering, the rusty springs moaning with the jolting of his body as he coughed the hours through.

Then as quietly as he had come, Hank left.

After "that soldier's" last visit, the old man suspected a conspiracy in the air. He was restless. His pile of rags lay in the corner of his room under a film of dust. All day he hugged close to the house, sitting in one room, then another, tapping his cane against the wall, staring at his bent wife as she moved through the rooms at her daily work. And when the postman appeared in the sun, dragging his load, the old man met him on the steps, his greedy, warped hand open. But the postman had had a little front-porch conference with Pearl about an old man who would be likely to be waiting for mail from distant, strange places, so it was given to Grandma, who hid it from him.

"He's trying to take my baby girl away from me!" groaned the old man.

"Ha!" Pearl rared back on her hips, and flipped her hands in their sockets. "Baby girl, my foot! A lot you care for baby-girl Pearl. It's the ol' bread and butter I lug out of me at that sewin machine you're worryin about. But Hank ain't stealin me away, so hush."

But he was. The quiet soldier was writing letters of maneuver. How to get her out of the house without causing panic. I often wondered what he'd do with her, a thirty-six-year-old virgin. He wasn't a grand prize himself, but she wasn't even cracker-jacks. Well, I suppose, if you're all alone some night with the cool keen ache of rain in your nostrils, and you start thinking of her down there inside that tall print dress . . . But a lifetime!

The fall came, and early snow.

The old man knew something was about to happen. They all did. They sat in a tight group in the evening, hidden behind love stories, knitting needles, self-conscious eyelids—and a thread of foreboding wound itself around their brains.

She told her mother, she told Thad, she told the postman, and my mother and me. But the old man had to figure it out alone, watching the turned-away eyes, the sidestep as one of us passed him, the awkward hands—a hundred other little things that mimicked his fear.

And he watched her, her restless body shifting inside her loose dress after a fresh bath, her ankles rubbing together, her fingers growing hot on the quick needles, her pale blue eyes narrowing on an image of some passionate night in a huge northern city. He knew. And he knew there was nothing he could do but whine and gripe and watch and wait. So he did.

They'd all prepared themselves for the time when it would happen, but when the time was there one morning and Pearl wasn't, they all realized they had prepared only in their minds, and that the future looked bleak, grinning at them like Emmett.

At four AM I was awakened by the coal trucks shifting into third as they set forth toward the morning light. Up on my elbows, I could see her standing on the corner, her face paled by the mist. The air pump ticked. I searched the shadows for Emmett, as though I expected him to be there, but he was nowhere. The bus stopped, the huge door swung open, and, not glancing back, she was received up into the beginning of distance.

That morning they woke up with sunlight on their beds and when they listened for the door to slam as Pearl went out to work, the only sound was the air-pump meter at the filling station beside the window, going ding-gock, ding-gock, ding-gock, on and on and on, as Buster pumped enlivening air into cold rubber tires.

They sat at the table, even the old man among them, spraying the white mugs of coffee from the fountain of his disease. No one said a word. They just looked at each other, their bellies like grey sun-flowers opening with hunger, their minds knowing better than to think.

And when the postman came, the old man was on the porch, but now he lacked a purpose for being there. After a while, Emmett came from behind the house and softly sat down beside him on the steps. He looked at Emmett for a long time. Then, just as the old woman came out to tell him his supper was ready, he got up and walked into the dense sedge field with *his* Emmett, whose face was, after all, a good face.

For weeks their lives were shadows, their talk was pale. Thad's one eye was getting worse. He had fits. He would run screaming through the house, blind, bursting his face against a wall. And after it was over and he lay on the floor, the old woman would kneel down and put her cool hands on his brow, whisper to him words neither of them heard. And the old man would lie in his own darkness.

Something went wrong with the air pump so that its ticking was louder than ever, louder than a fat clock. We lay inside our limp minds and listened to the bell, unable to sleep.

Then one day in the third week, when the sun was drawing its dull glow off the side of the house, a Trailways bus stopped at the corner, and Pearl stepped down into the grass.

It was not long until everything was the same as before Pearl had gone. The music of eating was no longer dull and soft, Thad's belch once again declared the end of each meal, and the old woman sat with that bland, pleased look on her face. But the old man was still afraid.

The snow disappeared and the buds nudged out of the choking bark. Flowers nodded at the sun, birds took the seed and left the fruit. Pearl was home and all was well in the world, it seemed, even if the meter was maddening, and Emmett wouldn't stay away.

Pearl was sitting on the steps with her knees up, writing paper braced on her lap. I was on the grass in a lawn chair below her, trying to read. The grass and the hot cement steamed from recent rain. I heard her pen on the paper, and felt her gaze go past me toward Buster, who was horsing around with loafers in front of the pumps.

"Pearl, how come you came back home? Everything's all right, isn't it?"

"Sure. Hank's a corporal now. We have an apartment. I'm gonna make some doilies for the doo-lally racks." I could hear her dress as she bent down close to my back. "Don't breathe a word about this, but I'm just staying a few months. You know—until Momma can get a job. Then I'm going back to my husband."

Neither of us breathed a word for a while.

"Say, Pearl?"

"Yeah?"

"Uh, tell me—how—how did it feel to you?"

My back was to her when I said it. Then I heard her heels strike the wood and her dress whispered. Then the screen door yawned open, and clapped shut. My face got hot and my stomach clenched into a wad, and all I heard was the air hose ticking behind me.

Very early one morning, as I was going down to stop the ticking, we met on the porch, me in my jock shorts, she in that mauve nightgown, and fog hugged our bodies. Our eyes met before we actually saw each other. There was nothing to do but go back in, because someone had silenced the ticking—with Kotex, I learned the next day.

I didn't ask her anything more about her married life.

The old woman came home one evening after her first trip to town in ten years. She had gotten a job in a button factory. She sat down in Pearl's soft, deep chair with her tiny grey hat askew, her ankles spilling over the sides of her dark shoes. She had a bag of buttons in her cupped hands.

"They give 'em to me, free."

The old man looked at the multicolored buttons. Then he looked at his wife. He went into his room and bolted the door.

Pearl chose to make her escape on a rainy morning in early November. I heard her go to the front door. I waited through the silence while she stood there looking out. Then I heard quick, quiet little noises coming from the rooms. There was no one else in the house, and she was packing. I could almost hear her breath.

She must have been very nervous. I kept hearing things strike the floor. I imagined a bead of sweat running like a burst seam down the inside of her leg. The screen door opened but it wasn't her. I heard the thump of a cane on the hall floor, the muffled *fuff* of his rag bag bumping against the wall.

"What are you doing, little girl?" yelled the throaty, broken voice. An animal moan rose on the hot air. "She's leaving her own father to die by ghosts in the dark! Do you want something to get me in that room some lonely night? Huh? Oh, my little baby, baby girl, please lay those black silk things back in the dresser. Please."

"Get out of here, Daddy! I'm going to my husband, I'm thirty-six and I've slaved enough. I want something that gives back what it takes. Now get the hell out of here, and stop slobbering on my shoulders."

"I won't let you go! This is your father talking to you, do you hear?"

"My father! Oh, my god, yes! Now, Dad, I said get away." The old man went into a fit of violent, shattering coughs. "Damn it, you got it on my mouth, you filthy—nasty—old man! Get in your room!"

A door slammed. A key clicked.

Bones barely covered with flesh struck the door again and again. It rattled in its frame. And the old man's voice sounded as though it came from a well. The screaming and the thin flesh striking wood went on for a long time. Then the front door slammed.

A Trailways bus plunged to a stop before the house, and Pearl stepped up out of the slush of melting snow into the mammoth iron brute that carried her northward just as a squad of jet planes zoomed above its broken, speeding shadow, the noise lingering over the house.

My hearing waned back to normal. The air meter's ticking droned, making the silence profound.

I sat there with a book limply in my hands, as though waiting, for what I didn't know. Then it became as clear as the glaring sunlight on the window sill. I was waiting for the screams, for the beating on the door, but silence and ticking was all I heard.

I was in the hall, staring into the dim, furnace-heated rooms before I realized that I was no longer sitting in my chair. I walked into the rooms as a solitary child enters the cemetery. The faucet was dripping in the kitchen. The curtains were motionless as granite. The mirror on the wall, a maze of sunlight, failed to attract my semblance. I put my ear against the door to the old man's room. The silence was a heartbeat of mute sounds.

I felt someone's hot breath on my neck, and it smelt foul. I swung my face around to meet a green-toothed grin. I didn't move, Emmett didn't move. I could not breathe for the foulness of his breath, and I was so terrified of his presence that I could move only as a mote drifting away in sunlight.

Finally, he moved away to another part of the room and my body slowly shed its rigidity. But when the loud, ear-bursting roar of the radio tore into my head, I ran from the house.

At the filling station, I 'phoned the hospital for an ambulance. As I nervously awaited its arrival, Buster said: "That ol' man sure likes his baseball, don't he? Sounds like he wants the whole world to hear."

The ambulance appeared as a sore eye on the crest of the hill.

As they carried the old man through the house, the men in fresh white uniforms looked furtively at Emmett's crouched figure, his ear pressed against the mouth of the loud radio. They were so nervous that when the crowd gave out with a terrific cheer, they nearly dropped the corpse as they carried him out to the polished red ambulance. This is a factory town, and soot fell like flies upon his white face and crossed hands.

I don't know whether they told Pearl. She didn't return for the funeral.

No one came. Except Emmett. He sat quietly on the porch. There were only a meager few flowers. Emmett came with long, nodding sedge-grass. The wind blew, the chill penetrated.

The next day the children in the neighborhood played funeral. Emmett was the corpse. When the mothers called the children in for fear of Emmett, he lay alone in the sunlight for a while under a heap of dead weeds. Then with the limp sedge dropping from his hair, his mouth, and his overalls, he rose and pushed his tire through the grass, leaving a whisper.

All winter, the old woman worked on in the factory, sorting buttons. At evening, I heard her feet scraping the sidewalk as she carefully plowed through the maze of children cluttering it. Fat hung over her ankles, lavender veins crawled up her legs, and her hair fell out. The light was being drawn out of her like money from a bank by a greedy kid. Then in April the factory shut down.

Throughout the day, Thad groped his dubious way through the house, or lay in the grass with his face to the ground, listening to the faint chatter of the insects of spring. Emmett would come and sit beside him and get him interested in making clover chains. After the chains were made, they didn't know what to do with them, so they left them there in the sun to dry up.

It got so Emmett was no longer merely tolerated in the house, but allowed and, finally, welcomed. The three of them sat around the living room with their hands in their laps. Emmett made up a lot of games, and each night there was a new one, because he couldn't remember the ones already played.

In one of the games they pulled all the shades and everyone sat on the floor in total darkness. Then Thad was secretly instructed by Emmett to go outside and stand at one of the windows. That done, Emmett made promises to the old woman, who got up and went to the window of her choice. The first shade she raised revealed her son grinning and laughing at her. The echoes of their voices spiraled up to my room where I was trying to read.

The terrible pain in Thad's head became unbearable. One day the old woman came home and told my mother that her boss had bought her house. She was going to use the money for surgery on Thad's eye.

In a few days some men in summer suits came into the house and bought all the furniture, leaving the old woman a bed in the room she had shared with Pearl, who never wrote.

That night I went with them when a neighbor drove Thad to the hospital. The old woman kissed his bearded cheek and handed him the baloney sandwiches she had fixed. We drove back to the house and what was said made no sense.

The old woman had stopped looking for a new job. She had grown too weak to work. She was going to leave come morning and stay with a relative.

Before daylight, I was awakened by the echo of loud, hysterical laughter, sounding as from a well. Recognizing it as the old woman's laughter, I grew rigid.

Wearing only my shorts, I went down to see what had come over her. I paused at the door, hearing the air-pump meter ding-gocking beneath the louder laughter. I opened the door.

The old woman's long gray hair whirled around her like a dull, tattered maypole, she lay in moonlight on a white sheet, writhing under Emmett's darting fingers as he followed with agility her tossing body.

I slammed the door and leaned heavily against the clammy wall.
They tore Pearl's house down.

The New Orleans of Possibilities

Rind mist prickling his nostrils, he crushed the orange slice against his palate, constricted his gullet to keep from swallowing too much of the surging juice at once, enjoyed even the sting where his new pipe had burnt the tip of his tongue.

"Where did you get this orange?" Kenneth asked the woman at the next table whose smile as she had offered him the fruit had enhanced the shockingly sudden deliciousness of the juice.

"At the produce market down the street," said the man, realizing the woman had not heard Kenneth, enrapt as she obviously was in the first hour of the Sunday morning of lovers.

"I haven't had a real orange in years," Kenneth said to the woman, who turned toward him, the breeze blowing her hair across her eyes. She smiled again, *for* him now.

Eating the orange, section by section, Kenneth glanced at the lovers, who, in their felicity, had chosen more strawberries, bananas, black cherries, peaches, and oranges than their stomachs could hold, whose overflow of felicity and fruit had touched him. So it was not only in balmy breeze and Sunday morning sunlight that they basked.

New Orleans, the most romantic city of his imagination, the city in which he had once expected to realize so many possibilities, had become so routine, he had awakened in the Royal Sonesta this morning to a palpable, almost urgent impulse to do something slightly unusual. Having supper alone at Begue's last night, on the occasion of his thirty-sixth birthday, he had realized that except for Charleston he had seen—though only as a salesman can see—every

American city he had ever wanted to see. Doubting there would ever be a necessity to go to Charleston and failing to imagine it as a vacation attraction for Helen and John made him sad. But up in the room, looking down on Bourbon Street, where he no longer felt safe walking at night, he had realized too that New Orleans, his favorite city even over San Francisco, had in his routine become almost as bland as an airport layover. And when the morning light woke him, he knew he had not felt merely the blues of a man away from home on his mid-passage birthday. He had projected his life to live in cities, and the cities were gone. Sipping *café au lait* with fifty tourists outside the Café du Monde and eating beignets had not quite met his criterion for something slightly unusual. The gift of the orange, the woman's smile, had.

The lovers left their table littered with fruit peelings, seeds, rinds, pits. Unable to sustain the shared moment in the breeze and sunlight, Kenneth walked toward the produce market, his system so unused to juice straight from the rind that he felt nauseated.

The second time he had come to New Orleans the heat, humidity, and pollution had been so intense he had seen the market from an air-conditioned touring bus with Helen and John. The first time, he had come alone to handle a new account and had confined his walking to Bourbon Street.

The mingled odors of fruits and vegetables were so intense that he tasted the market before he smelled it.

Walking under the long open-sided shed, down the narrow aisle between the stalls, Kenneth felt as if the bodies, faces, hands, and the fruit and vegetables were a palpitating morass that excited and delighted him, reminding him of his childhood birthday parties in Indiana. He bought pears, apples, peaches, bananas, a pineapple, strawberries, oranges, and tomatoes, and wondered what he would do with them. Appointments in Houston and Dallas lay between New Orleans and home. I may never *see* stuff like this again in my lifetime, he thought, smiling condescendingly at his isolated gesture.

Entering the lower end of the shed, he saw that this section was given over to a flea market. He wished Helen, who loved garage sales, could be there. The intriguingly slummy atmosphere of this part of the French Quarter, of the market, drew him among the tables, some of which were set up in the parking spaces. Bright old clothes hung from the barred windows of a discarded streetcar with Desire as its destination. Inside a high iron fence, tourists were being guided through the vast Old Mint building, recently restored after decades as a prison.

His mood fluctuated between revulsion at the sleaziness and excitement at possibilities. Looking at objects that ranged from cheap new pseudocraft products to genuine antiques, from trash to bizarre oddities of some value to collectors, he forgot the queasiness that *café au lait*, powdered-sugar–sprinkled beignets, and orange juice had induced. Realizing that he had fully acted on impulse to break routine and open himself to possibilities made him feel a sense of adventure, and a little anxiety—made him reach for objects he had never imagined he would ever want to look at, much less buy and use and enjoy.

"For the man who has everything," Helen had said, presenting the pipe three days before his birthday. Now he had twelve pipes, only one of which got the use and care a pipe demands. And here, too, among the disgorgings of New Orleans attics were discarded pipes that perhaps someone here would be glad to smoke.

That a buyer had been imagined for each likely and unlikely object on disarrayed display intrigued him as much as the objects themselves. The snaggle-toothed old woman, who looked like a caricature of a witch, had sat in a foul-smelling room somewhere in this sprawling city and imagined a buyer for those rusty iron pots. Kenneth paid her three-fifty for the cast-iron corn-stick mold, so heavy it almost balanced the load of fruit in his other hand.

And that bearded man, whose underarm stench, palpable as flesh, reached across the table, had stooped among those coils of barbed wire and anchors and canoe paddles, seeing buyers clearly enough to load it all into the back of his VW van and haul it down here at daybreak. Kenneth passed on by the barbed wire.

And this spaced-out girl, dark circles under her eyes, veinless smooth hands trembling more visibly than the old woman's, had squatted in some chairless, mattress-strewn, windowless slave quarters off a courtyard as sump-smelling as a Venice canal, convincing herself someone would buy one or two or three of the old photographs she had foraged out of attics and basements and rooms of abandoned houses, old houses torn down, and trash cans where she had hoped perhaps to find edibles. Too flummoxed by such incomprehensible assumptions to move on, Kenneth stopped, stared down into the lopsided cardboard box into which the girl had dumped thousands of photographs, mostly snapshots muted in time's sepia tone.

The moist fruit had dampened the bag. He lifted and hugged it, damp side against his coat, and walked on among the 78-rpm records, the fabrics and shirts and blouses and dresses, the rings and buttons, the glass insulators, the Mississippi driftwood and cypress knees, the old comic books, the tables of unfocusable clutter, the neater displays of antique toys, the moldy books and *National Geographic*s dating from the twenties, that Kenneth was too burdened to leaf through.

He made the rounds, continuing long after fatigue and nausea and the increasing heat and humidity had made him sluggish, as if to miss even scanning sight of any of this stuff would wake him in the middle of the night in Houston or Dallas or home in Chicago, regretful, with that gnawing sense of unfinished business. The peculiarness of such a premonition making him feel a need to assert his own control over his behavior, he turned away from the flimsier tables lined up alongside the streetcar named Desire, and with the phrase, *he retraced his steps*, consciously in his mind, went back the way he came.

Kenneth waited for a young man in overalls and wide-brimmed leather hat to pay for the photographs he had stuffed into his pockets.

"May I set these down a moment?" Kenneth looked at the dark circles around the girl's eyes. She nodded rapidly, unblinking.

He reached into the bulging box, asking, "How much are these?" to make conversation, for the girl made him uneasy. He picked one of the photographs gently from the clutter, as if handling someone's personal effects.

"Fifty cents a handful."

"You don't sell them one by one?"

"Fifty cents a handful."

Imagining the young man in overalls grabbing two fistfuls, cramming his pockets, crushing some of the photos, shocked Kenneth.

"Get out the pictures, Granny." His grandmother used to imitate the way he had said that when he was a boy. Then she would honor his new request and take the hat box down off the shelf in her closet and sit beside him on the couch and gently pick them one by one from the loose pile. He felt an urge to tell this girl what his grandmother said, to imitate *her* voice imitating his own, but even had she not stared at him, seeing nothing, he knew he wouldn't have told *any*body.

His fingers webbed together to cradle his head, a man leans back in a high-backed straight chair, his foot braced on a white railing that runs blurred out of the edge of the photograph toward the end of the porch, getting thinner as it reaches his foot, the toe of the other foot touching the floor almost delicately. Someone caught his semicandid pose at the turn of the century. The locale was possibly the Garden District. Smiling, imagining his grandmother's response Kenneth placed the photograph back on top, trying to put it where he found it.

He picked up a raw recruit of the forties, saluting, mock-serious, his billed cap resting on his ears. On V-J Day was he in Times Square or beneath a white headstone in France? He laid it down.

Propped up in a hospital bed, a young woman in a lace-trimmed nightgown holds her newborn baby. The kind of shot Kenneth had once snapped himself.

A plump man in suspenders sits in his favorite chair under a fringed lamp on a stand, his delicately smoking cigar held between the fingers of his up-raised hand, at the ready.

An old man changes a tire on a road in arid hills, a little boy sitting on the running board. The man's wife probably took this one. Out West, on vacation.

An elementary school class against a freshly washed blackboard, half of the children smiling, half tight-lipped. Losing their baby teeth?

A child sits on a table, a birthday cake with three candles between its legs, presents heaped on both sides. Kenneth had one of himself at four, a similar pose.

A young man in a jogging outfit, his arms full of old record albums, stopped to glance over Kenneth's shoulder at a family in their backyard under a mimosa tree, a man in hammock, a child in diapers wearing a sailor hat, lifting the long handle of a lawn mower, a woman taking a bite from a piece of cake, an old man reaching for an apple from a tree, smiling for the camera.

"You want that one, sir?"

"I'm just looking."

"Mind if I take it?"

"No, go ahead."

"Fifty cents a handful," the girl said, with no more response to the young man than to Kenneth, who was feeling older than thirty-six the longer he stood there.

The young man obediently grabbed "a handful" and carefully slipped them into the pocket where he had found the fifty-cent piece.

Kenneth wondered whether older people had bought any of the pictures. As he picked them up at an increasingly faster tempo, his assumption that they came from many sources was confirmed. The faces from picture to picture bore no resemblance to each other, although a few that turned up in succession were in a sequence. They seemed to span decades, with many settings beyond New Orleans. Kenneth looked at her. Maybe she wanders in a trance like a gypsy from city to city, rummaging in trash cans. A free romantic life, for which he felt a fleeting envy, irrational not only because she looked like death warmed over, but because "wandering from city to city" described his own life.

A young man and his date pose in formals at a prom. Kenneth wondered whether the slim young man now had a pot belly.

A telephone operator of the forties, surprised, ruins a candid shot, shouting no, her hand thrust out to blot the camera eye.

Children, perhaps a Sunday school class, at a picnic, one boy in a swimsuit, looking straight up into the sky. Kenneth imagined an airplane.

A grinning young man opens the door of his new, perhaps his first, car, early fifties model.

A man behind a soda fountain, his hand on the nozzle, two girls having turned from their sodas to smile at—good ol' George, Kenneth imagined. I can remember cool soda fountains, said Kenneth, almost aloud. Helen would get a kick out of this one. They were just going out when we came in.

"I'd like to buy this one."

"Fifty cents a handful."

"No, just this one. Glad to pay fifty cents for this one."

"Look, man, I'd like to dump all of this, save me the hassle of lugging it back to the room. Take a handful, will you?"

"Why not?" He pushed together, like strewn bridge cards, enough to stack on his right palm.

As he slipped the stack into his coat pocket, she said, still not looking at him, not seeing him, "Take two—no extra charge."

That would be greedy, he started to say, but the comment seemed inappropriate even for her benumbed ears. He started aligning another stack.

"Look, man, like they aren't going to bite you."

"No, I just . . ." He wondered how, in such situations, such marginal people manage to make one feel inept, inferior.

Digging down with a kind of venal abandon, Kenneth dredged up an overflowing handful, noticing that one of those that spilled was a snapshot of a young man sucking in his belly, flexing his muscles, letting his pants drop over his hips below his navel, clenching teeth and bugging eyes that were the spitting image of his own. He smiled self-consciously, as if the girl, her hand still held out for the fifty cents, had discerned the resemblance in the same instant of surprise.

Now what do you know abut that? Amazing. He'd always heard that by the law of averages there must be somewhere on the earth someone who exactly resembles yourself, and in all time and all the universe, someone who is your exact duplicate, or your *doppelgänger*, a scary concept that had universal appeal. And once, he had picked up the newspaper, startled at the face of a bush pilot who had crashed in the Alaskan wilds, survived subzero weather for five weeks, and lay in the hospital. Even with a tube up the nose, the frost-bitten face against the white pillow was so obviously his own, he called Helen out of the shower, dripping, to look at it. "That's Kenneth Howard all right," she corroborated.

Picking it up, recalling the girl's assurance it wouldn't bite, Kenneth started to slide it beneath the deck as a novelty item to startle Helen and John and party guests. Within the magnifying range of his first pair of glasses, the face proved to be Kenneth's own.

The exhilarating moment of discovering a wild coincidence faded quickly into reasonable doubt. He put the second deck in his other coat pocket and looked closely at the face. Holding his breath, his teeth clenched in a jack-o-lantern grin, his eyes bulging like Peter Lorre. Who could—could even he?—say whether the face was his. When? When he was about seventeen. Where? Against the side of a garage, the white paint peeling badly. He remembered his severe sunburn peeling that summer. But that was not his father's garage. Perhaps a neighbor's. He tried to remember, and couldn't. He looked for a scar or some revealing mark on his naked chest. All his scars dated from college football. Was that black spot the size of a nickel his navel? How does one recognize one's own navel? He laughed. But it didn't seem as funny as on the surface it ought to have. Well, it's not me.

Imagining the girl scrutinizing him for his strange behavior, Kenneth looked up. Still, she saw nothing—catatonic—her palm open, not impatiently. Indifferently.

Not possible. Not possible? Hadn't he always thought of New

Orleans as the city of possibilities? In New Orleans, what was not possible? Uneasily, he smiled, shrugged it off as a wild coincidence, the kind of experience you come to New Orleans for, even if you're coming anyway for routine reasons, and slipped the photo into his coat pocket with the others, wondering who had snapped this shot.

Idly, as he felt in his pocket for a fifty cent piece, he pushed his fingers through the box, stirring up images. He handed her two quarters and picked up the corn-stick mold. As he lifted it, the bag broke, and he had to chase the fruit down the aisle among shuffling feet. People helped him. It's the business suit. He remembered reading an article that answered the question, Who gets helped, where and when, if somebody drops something in a public place? Noticing that the oranges rolled the greater distance gave him a comforting sense of workaday reality. And there were the bananas lying where they had landed. None of the fruit was ruined except for several squashed peaches; rising imperceptibly, bruises would show hours later.

He eased his armload onto the table and walked briskly to the fruit and vegetable stalls and paid a dime for a paper bag. Walking back, the possibility struck him that if there was *one*, there could be another, perhaps others, in the bulging shapeless box, and he hurried to her table, afraid his fifty cents added to the day's take might have given her enough for a fix and she would be gone.

The girl, the box, the fruit were still there. He offered her an orange. She shook her head in revulsion.

The back of a man's head, severely barbered, as he leans away from the camera to kiss a woman, blotting out her face.

A woman smells a rose on a bush, wearing a flared hat of the forties.

A girl wearing a Keystone Cop hat and coat, a moustache pasted under her nose, thrusts herself toward a boy behind bars in a gag shot at an amusement park.

A formal gathering at an outdoor celebration of some sort—no, a funeral. Photographs *are* deceptive, Kenneth thought decisively.

Practicing, a majorette twirls her baton, fractioning her face.

A man washing his car. I think I know that guy. Kenneth set it aside.

A man working at his desk, looks up, smiles quizzically at the camera.

A sober-faced little girl pushes a toy, no, a regular baby carriage down a cracked sidewalk. Empty, or occupied?

His head turned, his eyes half-closed, his mouth oddly ajar, Kenneth, in an ambiguous setting, caught in a Polaroid shot, the surface poorly prepared by the chemical substance he almost smelled now. Cracking, scratched, perhaps by fingernails pawing over the contents of the box. Kenneth licked his lips. The eyes blurred, closing. Perhaps another—no, not another coincidence. He rejected the possibility that some submerged need in him was looking for resemblances. Letting the picture drop on the cast-iron corn-stick mold, he dug farther.

Firemen pose in front of a fire hall, standing, hanging all over a new engine, perhaps only freshly washed—yes, water sparkles, drips from the fenders.

A man, leering, pretends to sneak into an outhouse marked WOMEN.

A businessman, perhaps a government official, presents a check and a handshake to a well-dressed middle-aged woman.

A man strides down a crowded sidewalk, caught unaware in a shot obviously snapped by a sidewalk photographer.

A young man poses with his parents at a high-school graduation ceremony, the mother blurring herself as she moves toward her son, as if to kiss him.

A young woman sits in a swing, empty swings on each side, blowing cigarette smoke toward the camera.

If I find one more, just one more, then. . . . The third was clear, his face quite natural, the suit his first job suit, the setting unmistakably the front of the building, at the curb, beside the red, white, and blue mailbox and the *Keep Chicago Clean* courtesy trash receptacle. What was the occasion? Probably not his first day because he stood there (waiting for the light to turn green) with such aplomb, one hand in his pocket, the other casually holding a ciga-

rette at ease—obviously between puffs, not in a hurry, looking
straight into Kenneth's New Orleans stare, but not into the camera's
lens. Looking, like the girl, at nothing in particular, but unlike the
girl, so young and vibrantly alive and receptive, he struck Kenneth
as a charming, likable young man in his early twenties. He couldn't
see the street sign but he knew it was Halstead and Grand. When
was it taken? Who took it? The questions drew such total blanks, he
didn't start going over the possibilities. He wanted to dig for more.

One impression held his attention on the picture already in his
hand—he didn't seem to realize he was being photographed. He
looked at the Polaroid. Obviously candid. He pulled out the muscle-
flexing shot—even around this classic exhibitionist pose hovered a
sense of privacy violated. The show-off eyes were introspective. He set
the three aside, neatly together.

A man driving a tractor looks up as if responding reluctantly to a
request.

A stiffly posed, badly retouched color shot of a married couple.

An infant wearing a knitted tam manages a brilliant smile with
only a single tooth. The brilliance in the eyes. Was it still there?

A teen-age boy strains to pose for a self-portrait as he presses the
shutter release lever on the camera, seen in the lower right-hand corner of a bathroom mirror.

People in tennis togs crowd around as a man in a suit presents a
trophy to a man dressed for tennis. Kenneth thought one of the
spectators resembled a man he knew years ago.

Through glass from the rear, a shot of himself standing in an
empty room, his back to the camera, looking out a tall window in an
old house, wearing his football jersey, number 8. The stance, one
foot cocked back, his body leaning, his elbow propping it against
the window frame, his arm bent back so he could palm the back of
his head, the other hand in his pocket, was obviously not a conscious
pose for a photograph. He seemed to have been shot through a side
window at an angle that caught him looking out a front window.

The possibility that anyone he knew had taken these pictures
without his knowledge as a joke—they were not, except for the
muscle-flexing pose, gag pictures, and he remembered none of the

situations or occasions—was so remote, he left himself open to a
joking assumption the CIA had had him under surveillance since he
was seventeen—or maybe younger. He looked for younger shots.

A teen-age girl in shorts strikes a pinup pose against sheets on a
clothesline.

A man sets his face in a mindless expression for a passport or an
ID photo that has turned yellow.

Kenneth looked for someone he might know, even vaguely, in a
family-reunion grouping on steep front porch steps.

A woman and a boy pose in front of a monument, looking so inti-
mately at the photographer, Kenneth lucidly imagined the photographer himself.

A woman has turned from the trunk of a car, a sandwich held up
to her open mouth, four other people bent over, their backs toward
Kenneth, who, unable to see their faces, feels uneasy.

A double-exposed shot of Kenneth reading a newspaper on a
train, so intent upon a particular article he holds the paper and thus
his body at an awkward angle, giving the photographer an opening.
On the train window, as if it were a reflection, a child sits on a shet-
land pony. A Chicago train? Nothing showed to answer his question. He had ridden hundreds of trains, perhaps thousands.

He looked at the girl, wondering whether she might not suddenly
recognize him as a recurrent image in her scavenged collection. She
was still in a hypnotic world of her own making or of some chemical's conjuring. He took off his jacket, lapped it over the bag of
fruit, picked his sweat-saturated polyester shirt away from his skin,
wiped his hands along the sides of his pants, licked his lips again.
His mouth was too dry.

Kenneth began to dig into the box, shuffling quickly past the little brown studio portraits of the 1860s whose edges crumbled, leaving his fingertips gritty, past the baby pictures—in his mother's collection, he had never recognized himself—past the group pictures
that obviously excluded him, past the ones with spanish-moss back-
grounds, New Orleans settings, nothing specific to look for, his
breathing fitful against the expectation that each movement of his
hand would turn up out of this deep box his face. The savage's fear

that cameras snatched, photographs held the soul captive made Kenneth laugh at his own fearfulness.

A young man of the seventies sits in the grass on the levee playing a guitar, a barge passing behind him.

The rim of a pale shadow in bright sunlight smokes on a stucco wall, the partial outline of a camera looking as if it is attached to the photographer's hip.

A couple sit on a New Orleans streetcar, having exchanged hats, exhibiting beer cans.

A company picnic. Kenneth looked anxiously for someone he may have known at some phase of his life.

A man sleeps, perhaps pretends to sleep, in a fishnet hammock.

Kenneth is having lunch with a man whose fork obscures his face. Kenneth sits before his own plate as if wondering whether he can eat it all. Between himself and the man—he tried to recognize the ornate cuff links—communication has visibly ceased or not yet really begun, perhaps was never resumed. What restaurant was that? His memory responded to nothing in the decor. *November 1972* printed in the white margin stimulated nothing. It did not appear to be one of those restaurants where girls come around taking pictures of moments to be treasured forever. No third party had said, "Hold it! Smile! That's terrific!"

"Say, miss. . . . Say, miss?"

"Fifty cents a handful."

"I know, but I just wanted to—I just wondered—could you tell me where you collected these photographs?"

"I don't remember."

He showed her one of the pictures. "Do you have any more of this fellow here?"

He showed her the one of his back in the empty room.

"I don't know."

He showed her the one on the street corner. "Him. Recognize him?"

"No."

"Him?"

"No."

"How about him?"

"No."

"They're me. They're all me." He looked into her lackluster eyes. "See? Each one of them resembles me to a T. I mean, they *are* of me. Somebody took. . . . Do they look like me?"

She nodded, expressionless.

"Then do you remember where you first found them?"

"No."

"Do you remember when?"

"No."

Pigeons perch on a woman's arm, tourists feeding pigeons behind her, a European cathedral in the background.

A boy stands at attention to show off his new scout uniform.

An elderly couple stands in front of a tour bus, the letters spelling its destination backwards.

A religious ceremony, ambiguous.

A man shows a string of fish, a river flowing in the background.

A young man and a young woman sit on a diving board, in profile, looking away from the camera, squinting into the sun.

A little boy sits on a plank placed across the arms of a barber chair, obviously captured on the occasion of his first haircut.

Kenneth stands in line at an airport, the destination on the board unclear. He is lighting his pipe, his lips pursed on the stem. Another Polaroid. Between himself and the woman in front of him, a fat boy in shorts takes snapshots with a mini-camera. In the picture the boy snapped—of his mother, his father, his sister, his aunt, his teacher, his friend, a stranger who caught his eye—one could see perhaps the person who had taken Kenneth's. The combination of images—in hand and imagined—made him aware of the nausea again. He had to make it to a bathroom quick.

He riffled through the box, thinking, I'm missing some, I must be missing some—there's no system to what I'm doing. The pictures, too quickly scanned, spilled from his hands back into the shifting clutter out of which he had fished them. The sun, the nausea, the eyestrain in the bright polluted air made him too weak for the task of sorting them all out on the cramped table.

"Will you be here all day?"

The girl shrugged her shoulders, "Man, how do *I* know?"

"Here, I'll pay for these—I'm—I'll come back right away—here, let me take some more handfuls." He shoved a handful into his right pants pocket, spilling, another into his left pants pocket, spilling, into both his back pockets, his inside breast pockets, his shirt, worrying about the effect of his sweat on them, stuffed some into the bag with the fruit, picked up the ones he had spilled, and gave her five dollars.

"Keep the change and try to stay around awhile, I'll come right back." He turned, hugging the bag of fruit, carrying the corn-stick mold out through the stalls, the parking spaces, and went back to her. "Well, did you get them all in the same place?"

"No, man."

"The same town? New Orleans?"

"Yeah. Maybe. Take another handful at a discount. Only a quarter."

"I just hope you're still here. I want to go through them one by one, systematically."

He made a final effort to see a glimmer of recognition in her eyes, and failing, turned away again, feeling distance increase between himself and the box hunched on the table.

In the dirty narrow street he flagged a taxi.

Lying stripped to his briefs, on his bed in the Royal Sonesta, the nausea ebbing, the photographs spread around him, he said over and over, Who took these pictures?

As he named his brother, his sister, his mother, his father, his other relatives, Helen, John, and a combination of them to account for the variety, each possibility struck him as so absurd, the rapidity with which he rejected them made him pant in exasperation with himself for even considering them.

He scanned the pictures slowly, hoping to stop short at the face of someone who might have become somehow obsessed, a creepy child-hood friend, a spurned sweetheart, an oddball relative, or a deranged business associate.

Looking up at the ceiling, he saw himself in many places, at many periods in his life, all past his seventeenth year, but he saw no faces of likely secret photographers.

What happened to the people who had taken them, causing the pictures to end up in the New Orleans flea market?

Was this person or persons male or female? Young or old? A contemporary? Known to him? Known well? A mere acquaintance? A business rival? Or a stranger? Friend or stranger, loved one or enemy, his frustration, his helpless astonishment had a quality of zero that he felt in his bones.

In the batches he had snatched up at the last moment, he had found other shots of himself. He is gassing up the car at a self-service island. Sitting on the bench as a player. Having a drink, sitting on the patio. Waiting for his bags to show up at a carousel in an airport. Walking the dog. Looking at stills outside a movie theater. Sitting in a lobby, his face hidden by a newspaper, as if he were a private eye, but obviously himself. Caught taking trash down a driveway to the curb. Lighting a cigarette in a stadium with friends, their faces turned away from the camera. Doing what people in the other photographs did. Sometimes strangers in the frame with him, but most often alone. As if he were being contemplated.

Each of the snapshots declared at a glance that he had not posed the image he held in his hand. Several types of cameras had taken the pictures, a range of paper sizes, shapes, stocks had been used. The quality of the photography ranged from awful to professional. A few were dated by the processors, a few had been dated in pencil, perhaps by the same hand but not one he recognized. Age or neglect had yellowed some. The negatives of some had been scratched. Some were soiled, damaged. A few had tabs of fuzzy black paper or smears of rubber cement on the backs as if they had been preserved in a scrapbook, then ripped out and put away or discarded.

Some of the places he recognized but couldn't fix in time. For some, he determined a time, but was at a loss to name the place. Perhaps he, she, they had kept a record of the dates and the places. Sometimes, he even remembered generally how he had felt, once specifically (melancholy), but not the context.

Lying on the double bed as if on a rubber raft at sea, he tried to go over every possibility again, imposing a kind of system. But each sequence to which he tried to adhere was besieged by so many un-accounted-for possibilities and sheer impossibilities, he abandoned them and gave himself up to chance. If a photo was worth a thou-sand words, he needed the words for these, because, as a neutral voice told him, "The camera never lies."

He scrutinized each picture of himself for the third time, strain-ing his eyes to detect ghost images such as spiritualists and UFO enthusiasts claim to see, or as religious fervor discerns Christ's vis-age in commonplace photographs. He remembered reading about a news photographer who happened upon a wreck on the highway and who shot the scene too fast to distinguish faces until his own seventeen-year-old son's face became more and more distinct in the developing tray.

The bounce of the springs as he jumped off the bed spilled some of the pictures onto the carpet. As he picked them up, he realized that the almost reverent care he used came not from narcissism but from respect for the feelings of the person or group who, he was inclined to conclude, had pursued through the years an obsession to chronicle his life.

Returning to the Market, he caught a glimpse of the Sunday-morning lovers, hoped they would wave to him, but more than a hundred people milling about the flea-market tables distracted them.

The girl was gone, but behind the box a little black boy's head was visible from the eyes up, his hands clutching the top, as if he were guarding.

"Where's the lady?"

"You the man?"

"Yes, where did she go?"

"She split, man. Said, give me a dollar for this box of pictures and a man come in a business suit give you a million dollars for this ol' box of trash."

"Here's two tens. Okay?"

"Man, that trash belong to *you*." He took the two tens and shoved the box toward Kenneth.

Kenneth picked up the box, looked around for any strays, and turned, lifting his knee to balance, as he embraced the shifting bulky sides of the torn cardboard box, feeling mingled awe and anxiety, remembering the two men who had bought pictures, feeling an impulse to track them down, wondering whether and from what angle sudden light was for a fraction of an instant flooding a dark chamber, etching his struggle on sensitized paper.

The Cartridge Belt

"Sergeant Brasbee," I said, "somebody stold my cartridge belt."

Under his blue cadre helmet liner that made him look like an anemic turkey with a bowl on its head, Field First Sergeant Brasbee smiled. "You are out of uniform, Hutchfield."

"Well, that's why I'm reporting somebody stold my cartridge belt, 'cause I know it's against regulations to be out of uniform."

Brasbee gimleted his eyes, pooched his thin lips tightly, swung around to face the troops in formation: "Men! Hutchfield claims one a you's a thief!" The least offensive approach I could have expected.

"Ah, hell fire, Hutchfield!" somebody yelled from the ranks. "Knock it off! This sun's boilin' hot!"

Executing a smart about face, Brasbee looked down at me again, as I began to cool in the shade his skinny shadow made.

"You *will* sign a statement of charges, soldier."

"You ordered us to stack arms, Sergeant." Noticing the men shifting sullenly in the sand, I stepped out of the shade Brasbee cast and squinted against the glare of the sun. "You posted no guard. So, the way they taught me the book in basic, it's your responsibility either to track down my cartridge belt—"

"It ain't *your* cartridge belt, soldier. It's government e-shoo. Just like *you* are."

"—or pay for a new one yourself."

"*Me?*" Bent at the waist, tapping his chest, he was almost as short as I am.

"And I'm not a government issue."

"In formation, soldier!" When somebody crossed, contradicted, or questioned Brasbee, his high, thin voice quivered hysterically. I always half-expected his dead pan to crack into a grin, finally admitting he was putting on an act. "Move 'em out, Corporal!" Brasbee ordered Stinnet, the Negro cadre who usually marched us in to lunch.

Stinnet was straight faced, too, but a deliberate comic, his mouth always hanging open in a slack-jawed, half-assed grin. He had a trick of breaking a long marching silence suddenly with a cadence call just enough *off* to make us shift to hit it right.

I always brought up the rear because of weak feet. I wore metatarsal bars on my combat boots, a revival in the army of a corrective measure I had needed from my freshman year in high school until I began sailing in the merchant marines. The bars augmented the success of surgery on my feet to correct a tendency to *Friedreich's ataxia*, or claw-foot deformity. And, I had a psychological block to moving left or right in unison with others on command. I moved readily enough but not always in the direction ordered.

"Hut, tew, threet, hoor, Hutch-field keep in step! Hut, tew, threet, hoor, Hutch-field keep in step!"

Back in the company area, as the men ran screaming like a hundred new species of birds and animals toward the mess hall to get close to the food they would have to gag down, I went into our tent-roofed cabin and took a thick brown-covered government transcript out of my footlocker. At the tail-end of the chow line, I picked up where I had left off that morning. "What you reading, Hutchfield?" the men had asked, the day it came in the mail, and when I said, "Transcript of the Rosenberg trial," in a voice that assumed they knew who the Rosenbergs were, they shut up, since most of them had had a few years of college and didn't want to betray their ignorance. At the University of Tennessee, I had often argued the injustice of the Rosenbergs' sentence, and one Sunday morning, I bought a Chilean newspaper in the small Andean village of Tal Tal and opened the photogravure section to a sepia-tone picture of Julius and Ethel in their coffins; I was shocked that the United States had gone through with the executions. Now that they were dead issues,

I felt a compulsion to know the facts. (I never finished reading the trial transcript.)

"Hey, Hutchfield," said Puckett, a freckled redhead from Alabama, "Brasso's really out to *get* your ass *this* time!" (Brasbee's fanaticism on the subject of buckle polishing had earned him the nickname 'Brasso.')

I had heard that line before—other companies, other names—but it always threw me, because who would know that better than *I* did, so I would assume the guy who yelled it had some inside information on a new charge. But it had been only five minutes since formation broke.

"Why not just take somebody else's belt at the afternoon formation?" asked Rastelli, a friendly New Orleans Italian who had become a student of my encounters with the army.

"I don't like stealing," I said, for the benefit of all listeners.

"It's not exactly stealing, Hutchfield. Half the company's been doing exactly that for two weeks."

"I know." I had watched the process daily, disgusted since the first man wandered around asking if anybody had seen a stray cartridge belt.

"He *can't* do it now, because he's already reported it stolen," said Puckett. "If you'd just kept your mouth shut like everybody else, and gone ahead and taken one when we fell in, you wouldn't have any problem."

"The problem started when the first man took his buddy's belt," I said, sensing that deep down they respected the concept of the buddy system.

"You don't think it was anybody in the company the *first* time, do you?" asked McFarland, a skinny, buck-toothed blond from Jackson, Mississippi. "We were all *in* uniform when we marched out of the company area."

"While we were in the building, somebody must have snuck up on the porch," said Puckett, imitating the action, "and slipped it off the blamed hook."

"Right," I said. "Then the victim should have reported it, because it was Brasbee's fault for not posting a guard."

"But that's too much trouble, Hutchfield," said McFarland. "What the hell's a little ol' cartridge belt?"

"It's not the damn cartridge belt that counts. What bothers me is that at every formation, twice a day for about two weeks, a new man becomes a thief."

"You calling *me* a thief?"

"Hell, *I used* to be—when I was little—stold a lot of stuff. Almost got sent to reform school. Both my brothers *are* in prison, *right now*." I said. "I send them money out of my measly pay check."

"How come you to quit?"

"Got saved. In a sawdust revival tent."

"You don't talk Christian to *me*," said Baggett, who had been mesmerized by a *Sheila of the Jungle* funny book.

"I'm not. I'm an agnostic, by god."

"An ag who?"

"A person who doesn't know whether there's a god or not."

"What the hell . . . well, you believe in Jesus Christ, don't you?"

"I like him, but I don't believe he was the son of God."

"What?" Baggett strangled the funny book. "You don't believe in no motherfucking Christ?"

"No, but maybe your example'll persuade me."

"I hope Brasso gets your ass courtmartialed."

"He'll play hell," I said.

I was sitting with Jesse, a Negro from Alabama who slept on the bunk above mine, when Brasbee walked by carrying his tray. "The supply sergeant said he'd open up five minutes early so's you can sign that statement of charges."

I didn't reply. He dumped his garbage and went out.

At five to one by my gold-plated, radium-dialed Elgin watch that I bought when I was an usher at the Bijou when I was twelve years old, I saw Sergeant Marcos, a handsome but surly young Greek with curly black hair, climb the steep steps of the supply building that sat on a rise above the tents in the shade of three tall pines.

As we stood in formation five minutes later, waiting for Master Sergeant Garrett to receive the roll report, I saw Marcos standing half in the cool supply room and half on the bright top step, looking down at me where I stood in the sand under the 102-degree sun.

"All present 'counted for, surp!" reported Sergeant Dunn. A big, tough, heavy red-faced fellow just back from combat in Korea, he hated my guts double when he learned we were related in a half-assed way, through my step-grandfather Chief Burnett of the Oak Ridge fire department, a man he disliked anyway, because the chief had risen in the world on a third-grade education, higher than Dunn, who was a fifth-grade graduate. My two years of college stuck in Dunn's craw like week-old cornbread.

"Sergeant," said Brasbee, "you got a man in your platoon's out of uniform"—in a tone as if he had told him that ten times before, but was only patiently reminding him again.

Sergeant Dunn did an about-face and walked among us. "'I God," he said, looking down the squad line at me as I looked straight ahead. "I might a knowed id be you, Hutchfield! Where's your god-damned cartridge belt?"

"Somebody stold it, Sergeant."

"Why didn't you *re*port it?"

"I did, but Sergeant Brasbee said—"

"Well, go sign a statement of charges for another one. On the damned double!"

"Can't, Sergeant," I said, suspecting that he was only pretending not to have heard about the missing belt at chow. "Wasn't my fault."

"Let's have the report, Sergeant," said Master Sergeant Garrett, a fat balding man.

Field First Brasbee twisted off an about-face, rendered a salute, and yelled, "All present and accounted for, surp!"

Sergeant Keats, a short, lithe, handsome fellow with a swooping blond pompadour, marched us out of the area. With Dunn, Keats had just returned from Korea. While the platoons passed by me, as I stood at attention, waiting to take up the rear, I always savored a few moments of separateness and freedom.

Brasbee stepped up behind me, saying, "Hutchfield, when you

fall out this afternoon, I want you to jerk one of those fuckin' cartridge belts off the hook."

"If somebody was to *add* one while I'm inside," I said, "that
would solve *every*body's problems."

Not until I'd marched off to take up the rear did he figure that one
out.

"You better shape up or ship out!" yelled Brasbee, lamely. "I got
your name, Hutchfield!"

"Hutchfield, get in formation!" Unlike Stinnet, Keats had no
sense of humor, and called cadence in strict military fashion.

Before returning to school, we had the week's indoctrination session in a building on a high sandy hill. After Sergeant Keats had
trounced down the eroded hillside and started off across the field
among bunches of tall, tough grass, he reminded me of Alan Ladd,
riding away at the end of *Shane*.

"Come back, Shane!" I called. "Come back!" Just as he turned,
the laughter of the men reached him.

"Who said that?" he yelled, looking up at us.

"Brandon de Wilde," said Jesse, who had seen *Shane* with me on
post the Saturday before.

"Better shape up!"

When he had gone too far to be likely to turn back and march us
up and down in the sun, I yelled, and the others joined in, "Come
back, Shane! Shane, come back!" imitating Brandon de Wilde.

When we came out an hour later, Stinnet emerged from under the
building raised on exposed brick pillars, where he'd dozed in the
shade, to march us over to the afternoon session of clerk-typist
school.

"Hut, tew, threet, hoor, Hutch-field keep in step! Hut, tew,
threet, hoor, Hutch-field keep in step!"

We were nearing the end of our six-week course, so the typing
instructor said, "Now today, gentlemen, I want you to write me an
essay right on your typewriters and hand it in. Make it as neat as you
can. You *will* be graded. But I'm giving you the freedom to write
whatever you want to. Just keep it clean."

They all laughed.

I spent most of the breaks composing poems and scenes and epiphanies for short stories on the backs of various forms we had to learn to cope with. But now I felt as if the army had shown an interest in what was really on my mind. I wanted to give the army something to think about.

> The paranoid is one of the most interesting of all psychotics, especially he whose complex exhibits the symptoms in their classic form. The most remarkable characteristic of paranoia that distinguishes it from most other psychological, or if you prefer, psychosomatic disorders, is the patient's level of intelligence, often far above that of the average person, and his use of almost flawless logic in explicating systematically the particulars of his persecution delusion. He builds from the raw material of his delusion an edifice far more elaborate than the most accomplished liar.
>
> A friend of mine, an atheist, made the remark one day in the course of a discussion of religion, "It seems to me not remarkable at all what Christ did. Isn't it clear that he was a hopeless paranoid homosexual?" The content of this striking statement, even from an atheist, interested me for a reason out of its context. I had cause to believe that my friend was not so well informed in psychiatry that he could know of the strong homosexual compulsion which has been discovered to exist working subconsciously in the mind of the paranoid. That my friend used the two psychoses, commonly referred to separately, in conjunction, impressed me that the relationship isn't quite as obscure as is sometimes suspected. The remark turned my mind to the case of Jesus Christ himself. I wondered what my friend's line of reasoning might be. Questions arose.

I tried, in the rest of the brief essay, to follow that line of reasoning, using a kind of Socratic method of interrogation. I still have the first draft. The finished copy was turned over to the Negro captain, a criminologist in civilian life, who headed the school.

A private named Howie, a slightly effeminate precocious Harvard

freshman majoring in philology, often talked with me in the post
library. Because his father was a friend of the regimental colonel,
Howie was often invited to cocktail parties and he told me that my
essay was the topic of discussion for weeks among the officers.

"Hutchfield, you are out of uniform!" screeched Brasbee, when
we fell in after school was out.

"You didn't have any luck tracking down my cartridge belt?"

"*I* ain't tracking down snake shit, soldier. Now, you got two minutes to break formation when we get back to the company area and
sign a damn statement of charges and get issued a by god new cartridge belt and fall back in formation for *re*treat. If I have to report
you out of uniform at *re*treat, your ass belongs to me, Hutchfield.
Two minutes!"

"That's two minutes wasted, Sergeant."

"You still claim one of your buddies is a mullifuckin' thief?"

"Whether he fucks his mother is a private matter." I hated that
expression.

"All right, by god! 'Ten-*hut*!" Brasbee waited a minute. "All
right, men, Ali Baba says one of you forty thieves rogued his cartridge belt. Now we're gonna stand here at attention in the blazing
ass sun until the one that done it fesses up."

Brasbee and Stinnet loped over and sat on the porch steps out of
the sun and fixed us in a double stare.

In three months, I had tangled assholes with the army on many
occasions, but I had never caused others to suffer for my own causes.
And I had never really hated comical Sergeant Brasbee until now, as
I stood there in the sun, feeling the hostility of the men sizzle
around me. They began to grumble and some shot whispered demands and threats to me to sign. Silently, I recited, "I moved
among them, but was not of them," and "The laws of God, the laws
of Man, he may keep them who will and can," and "Whose woods
these are, I think I know. . . ."

All around me in the blistering sun the men stood rigidly at attention, their minds working in the same way others had worked in

basic when, two weeks from the end of the cycle, we were ordered to report to the company commander to sign a loyalty oath that Senator Joseph McCarthy had forced upon the army. Since there had been no question in their own minds of their loyalty, few of the men had even read the document, fewer still read the attorney general's list, in fine print, of subversive organizations, mostly Communist or Communist front. "Have you ever sympathized with the aims of any of these organizations?" That was what caught *me*. I had never *belonged* to *any* organization, not even the Boy Scouts. But I sympathized with the ideal concepts of communism—just as many of the boys in the barracks sympathized rather violently with the practical actions of the Ku Klux Klan. When I pointed out that the Klan was on the subversive list, eyes narrowed, mouths clenched, bodies flexed, and I almost got my ass smeared. I refused to sign the loyalty oath, and while the McCarthy hearings were being televised in the dayroom every evening, I was being investigated by the Central Intelligence Corps. That was at Camp Gordon.

Every few minutes Brasbee stood up on the steps and yelled, "All right, the pig-hopper that done it better confess or ever' swinging dick *will* stand here till the dew falls."

But after ten minutes, he must have worried about us not showing up for retreat, because he stepped down and yelled, "Okay, move 'em out! On the double!"

When we hit tent city, Brasbee slowed us down to a march and Stinnet opened us up in song. "When I die on a Russian Front, wrap me up in a Russian cunt! Sound off! One, two! Sound off! One, two, three, four. . . . One, two!"

As I stepped off the blacktop, bringing up the rear, and marched between the two pines that bordered the sandy entrance to the company area, Sergeant Major Garrett violently pushed open the orderly room door and jabbed his fists into his fat hips. What he hated worse than listening to us sing cadence was to see us come in late.

Dunn and the other platoon sergeants stepped out from under the narrow eaves of the tent cabins and jumped down the short bank to the parade ground.

Breathless, drenched in sweat, we watched Lieutenant Glass, a tall slender Negro from Arkansas, step out of the orderly room, looking sharp, crisp, cool.

I liked Lieutenant Glass's walk, his sudden white smile. I imagined that when the cartridge belt incident came to his attention, he would resolve it justly. I refused to use the men's nickname for him, "Oily-tongue"—assigned because he often mispronounced words such as "Souse Carolinas."

As the squad leaders, platoon sergeants, and Field First Brasbee made their reports to each other up the chain of command (which a chaplain once told us went right on up to God) I thought maybe the cadre would keep the incident from Lieutenant Glass and that they would try to wear me down.

But Lieutenant Glass's sharp eye noticed me, and in a normal, clear voice, he said, "Sergeant Major, there is a man out of uneeform."

Sergeant Major Garrett did an about-face. "Man out of uniform!" he yelled, as if it were inevitable.

The other sergeants didn't even pretend to inspect their men.

"Private Hutchfield, sir," said Sergeant Dunn, as if to say, "Who else?"

"Have that man sign a statement of charges," said Sergeant Garrett, in a bored, it-shall-be-done voice. "And issue him a new cartridge belt."

After retreat had sounded over the Fort Jackson loudspeakers, and Lieutenant Glass had turned the company back to the sergeant major and his cadre, Sergeant Dunn commanded, "Hutchfield, step forward! Platoon, dismissed!"

Our platoon was first in the run for chow.

At attention, I looked up at Dunn.

"Hutchfield, for being out of uniform, you *will* report to the mess sergeant after chow. And you gonna ride that motherhumping range every night until you stand formation *in* uniform."

"Why?"

"Why, what?"

"Why do I have to ride the range? It wasn't my fault somebody stold my cartridge belt. Sergeant Brasbee ordered us to stack arms and he failed to post a guard. Put *him* on KP."

"You a real smart-ass, ain't you, Hutchfield? You better be glad this ain't Ko-rea. You wouldn't last a week."

"Heard they throwed your ass on KP," said Carter, one of my tent mates, on normal KP roster for the day.

"Yeah," I said.

"Young soldier, you better shape the hell up. Ol' Dunn's after your ass."

"Why don't you go ahead and sign, Hutchfield?" asked Puckett. "Lost mine on maneuvers in basic one time. All the hell they charged me was a dollar and eleven cents."

"It's not the money. How can a bunch of guys who steal from each other fight together? And for what?" I really wanted to know. They weren't interested in discussing it, not even academically.

"You're crazy, Hutchfield. You ought to be teaching Sunday school."

"He ort to have his nuts cut out," said Baggett, looking up from the same funny book.

"I don't see why we have to wear cartridge belts anyhow," said Jesse, sullenly.

"Yeah, what use are they?" asked Rastelli. "Did you ever *see* a cartridge in a cartridge belt?"

"Technically," said Puckett, "it's so when we march, we're under arms."

"You got any more of them silly reasons?" asked Jesse.

"See, you guys agree it's stupid," I said. "So why do you wear them? Why don't we *all* just turn up without cartridge belts, then maybe they'll see how silly it is."

"I ain't getting *my* ass throwed on KP. Ain't worth it."

That night, the mess sergeant made me wash the walls of the mess hall. A little before midnight, he released me. By the time I had walked, feet and legs so sore I could hardly move, through two company areas where men slept tight, crossed the blacktop into the swamp, I was twenty-one years old.

I followed a road of white sand into the swamp and stripped and, inspired by the soldier in Carson McCullers' *Reflections in a Golden Eye*, ran naked through the trees and vines.

"Sergeant," said Lieutenant Glass, in his quiet, penetrating voice, "there's a man in the ranks out of unee-form!"

When Sergeant Dunn couldn't believe his ears, he turned his eyes on me, and sure enough, I was out of uniform. Officially, not even the fatigues I had on were a uniform, for they were streaked with soot and soiled from the grease trap the mess sergeant had ordered me to clean.

"I want that man's name."

"Man out of uniform is Private Hutchfield, sir."

"Why isn't he wearing a cartridge belt?"

"Says he lost it, sir."

"It was stolen," I said.

The platoon groaned.

"Why is his uniform dirty and wrinkled, Sergeant Dunn?"

"He ain't too good at personal grooming, sir."

"I had to ride the range last night and—"

"Silence in the ranks!" yelled Sergeant Major Garrett.

"—then the washhouse was off limits."

"Nobody gave you permission to be at ease, soldier," said Lieutenant Glass. "Sergeant Major, I will inspect the ranks after chow, this morning. Every man *will* be in uniform. I don't want to see no discrapincies!"

My platoon snickered.

A little while later, I was standing at the urinal. Suddenly, Sergeant Dunn was right beside me.

"You wanna ride that black-ass range again tonight?"

"No."

"Supply Sergeant's opening up early."

"Sorry, Sergeant, I'm not going to sign."

"You fuck up my goddamn platoon, you fuckin' with *me*, soldier. I better not catch you out in Columbia. You lucky you got out of

Camp Gordon alive, boy. I got friends was with me in Ko-rea down there. They told me all about you, you dirty little commie!"

Dunn violently shook the drops off the end of his prong, shoved it in his pants, and walked out, buttoning up.

In the chow line and at the table where I sat and from tables nearby, I got a barrage of advice, all of it the same caliber.

After chow, Lieutenant Glass inspected the ranks. A lot of guys needed haircuts. Some of them needed to use Brasso on their buckles. "I got your name, soldier!" Brasbee had repeated occasion to say.

Lieutenant Glass stopped in front of me. "Sergeant, wasn't this man told to sign a statemint of charges?"

"Yes, sir. I told him yesterday at noon formation. He refuses." Brasbee held his clipboard braced between his forearm and his hip, waiting.

"He refuses?" Lieutenant Glass's small, bony, rather handsome face was only a few feet from mine, looking down at me. It was odd to be discussed as if I were invisible.

"I reported it—"

"Who give you permission to speak?" asked Brasbee.

Lieutenant Glass said, "Have Private Hutchfield sign a statemint of charges," and moved on, pretending to inspect the rest of the platoon, the last on his tour, moving more quickly, until the front rank must have seemed like striding past a picket fence.

As we were marching out of the company area, shepherded by Sergeant Keats, I noticed Sergeant Major Garrett deployed in front of the orderly room door, his fists stuck in the fat of his hips; behind him was the sign I had painted for him several weeks before with its misspelled word that had proved to him that I was, just as he had thought, an educated fool.

"Hutchfield, step out!"

I followed him into the orderly room. Through the window screen, I watched the others march on down the street.

"Hutchfield," said Garrett, pointing a loaded finger between my eyes, "you better shape up! You ain't gonna disrupt my company *no more*."

"I tried to do the right thing when I reported the theft to—"

"Don't you sass *me*. Soldier, when you talk to *me*, you keep your mouth shut."

Garrett told me Lieutenant Glass was very upset and that I had better sign right now and be in uniform for the next formation. I told him I wanted to be in uniform, but that I couldn't until Sergeant Brasbee recovered my belt.

"Come with me!" Sergeant Garrett chugged like a locomotive out the side door and straight up the steep path to the front steps of the supply room.

Sergeant Marcos stepped up to the counter, grinning, expectantly.

"Sergeant, issue this man a cartridge belt."

Marcos grinned. "He ain't signed a statemint of charges yet."

"Come on, come on."

Marcos slung a new, fresh-smelling belt on the table.

"Put it on." I strapped it on, warily, allowing the feeling of triumph to rise. It fell when he said, "Marcos, where's that statement of charges?" Marcos put it on the counter. "Now, *sign* that motherfuckin' thing."

"I'd sign it," I said, disgusted, as I always was, with that expression, "if I thought it would turn right around and fuck somebody's mother."

"A smart ass to the end," said Marcos, not grinning.

"This isn't the end. I'm not signing."

"You refuse an order?"

"This order, yes, because it's illegal."

"Take off that cartridge belt."

I unstrapped and draped it over the counter but it slithered off. I picked it up and put it down and Marcos snatched it up.

I followed the sergeant major out the door. He was storming down the path into the orderly room. Through the screen, shading my eyes with my hands, I said, "What do I do now, Sergeant?"

"Report to the clerk-typist school. On the double!"

As I walked past the window at the back of his chair, he swiveled and yelled, "On the *double*, Hutchfield!"

On the blacktop at the crest of a rise in tent city, I saw Sergeant Keats striding toward me through heat waves, pointing his finger.

"You the one that started them calling me Shane and mooing at me when I walk away," he said.

"You do look like Alan Ladd, Sergeant."

"You gonna look like a sieve tomorrow when I get you on that rifle range."

"Already had that in basic."

"You gotta requalify every six weeks, soldier. *I* requalified every day in Korea shootin' me some gooks."

In typing class, during the break, I worked out some futuristic ideas I had developed while cleaning out the grease trap the night before.

> After the ravages of war are cleared from the face of the earth and this final disfiguration passes into the bloody pages of pre-Communist history, Mankind will move on in sublimity toward its destiny. It is not Russia who rules the world today. It is the people everywhere who rule. When America surrendered, Russia's role in the struggle for universal freedom played out, and she ceased to exist as a nation. Comrades, nations no longer exist anywhere in the world—there are now cities and countries within the world community. Never again will one nation wage war with another, simply because nations no longer exist. The factories of the world that produced bombs during the war will tomorrow provide the wretched of the world family with clothing, shoes, and means for construction. Out of tanks, we, each of us, working together in a labor of love and need, will make bridges and cars, and from battleships will come the everyday items with which to make life and work more pleasant. In a matter of a year, Comrades, not a single piece of war mechanism will exist to offend your eyes and enrage you at the stupidity of man.
>
> Never before has man been given or rather given himself the opportunity that today is his—that of shaping

out of chaos with the technology war can't erase a new, abundant, free, happy world.

At formation, nothing was said about my being out of uniform. Nor when we returned to the company area. But at formation after noon chow, Sergeant Dunn told me to report to the mess sergeant for KP after supper—punishment for wearing dirty fatigues, which "shows disrespect for the uniform of the United States Army."

That afternoon, Sergeant Major Garrett stood in for Lieutenant Glass at retreat. His absence and no mention of the cartridge belt made me feel the conflict was over, but still, I felt a little uneasy.

That night, I was cleaning out the giant cookstoves, when Brasbee stuck his helmeted head in the door and yelled, "Hutchfield!"

"Here!"

"Report to the orderly room on the double!"

I double-timed it to the orderly room. The night orderly told me, "Report to the company commander."

Lieutenant Glass lived off post. What the hell was he doing in the area this late at night? I knocked on his door.

"Come in."

Absorbed in a big thick book, he pretended to be oblivious to my presence. Facing me on his desk was a statement of charges, my name typed in.

"Private Hutchfield reporting to the company commander as ordered, sir." The tribal way to pronounce "sir" on such occasions was 'surp,' but I liked the lieutenant and meant him no disrespect.

"At ease, Private Hutchfield." He had a soft, gentle voice. On that hot August night, I felt in the room, with its mellow lamplight, a certain intimacy. A young white southern liberal and a Negro from Arkansas. We could talk now and he would understand.

We did talk, quietly, logically, coolly, and I even threw in a few parallels between my collisions with the army and the injustices perpetrated against his people, many of them daily little assaults on their dignity, selfhood. But if he understood as a Negro, he refused, as an officer, to accept the consequences of my reasoning, which, I figured out later, would mean his undermining the authority of his cadre, contributing to their defeat in the eyes of all those educated young men. The cadre was made up of grammar school and high school dropouts who had served their country in World War II or Korea. Bigger things than a cartridge belt had been at stake. I realized that. I did not scorn it.

I knew it was a trivial matter, but I was also convinced that to sign that statement of charges would be the first step toward becoming a casualty in my private war with the army. When the next small issue turned up, I could hardly resist on principle, and one small, trivial issue after another would follow, and then, some time after I had ceased to split hairs or care, a major act of capitulation.

Lieutenant Glass told me to sign the statement of charges.

I refused.

I had never heard of anyone refusing to sign a statement of charges; although I had heard that a few others had refused to sign McCarthy's loyalty oath, I had never met any of those men. I felt scared and alone, standing there in that office, as Lieutenant Glass slammed the big red book shut and let it drop melodramatically on the desk.

Without raising his voice, but with a quiver of suppressed rage, he said, "Hutchfield, I can have you court-martialed on five separate counts—maybe six. Repeatitly showing disrespect for the uniform of the United States Army, repeatitly refusing to obey the commands of non-commissioned officers, repeatit insubordination, negligent loss of governmint property, and repeatitly appearing in fo'mation out of unee-form."

"What's the sixth one?"

"Refusing to obey a direct order from your commanding officer."

"But you haven't given me a direct order, sir."

"I am now."

"You're giving me a direct order to sign a statement of charges?"

"That's right. I order you, Private Hutchfield, to sign that statemint of charges."

Knowing that refusal to obey a direct order from one's commanding officer carried a severe penalty, I asked, "Where's a pen, sir?"

Smiling, he pulled a green fountain pen out of his middle drawer, uncapped and handed it to me. I noticed it was just like the one my modern poetry teacher had given me when I went into the merchant marines and that I filled with green ink and used to write poems and stories and philosophical reflections and had lost in a whorehouse in Antofagasta, Chile, the year before.

But it wouldn't write. I looked up, smiling. "Ironic, isn't it, sir? Out of ink."

In no mood for irony, he snatched it from my hand. "It can be filled with ink."

But ink won't come out of a khaki shirt. Looking down at the black ink he had squirted, he cursed under his breath. Now, his wife, too, would hate me.

I signed with a flourish.

"A new cartridge belt will be ee-shooed to you at the supply room in the morning after reveille. That's all."

"Yes, sir."

I returned to KP just as the boys on the regular roster were leaving. The mess sergeant was a red-headed, good-hearted old fellow about to retire.

"I left a light on for you, son. Sergeant Dunn said for me to save mopping the floor for *you*. I'm going to bed. Just lock up when you get done."

I took off all my clothes and mopped the floor, sweat streaming down from my scalp to my ankles. And then I got a huge round pot, filled it with cold water and dumped it over my head. The shock almost made me faint.

"Man in the ranks out of uniform!" yelled Sergeant Brasbee.

Lieutenant Glass's face was stunned blank.

"Hutchfield!" screamed Sergeant Major Garrett. "You was supposed to report to the supply sergeant right after chow this morning!"

"I did as I was ordered. I signed a statement of charges. But Lieutenant Glass *didn't* give me a direct order to appear in full uniform."

Lieutenant Glass saluted the sergeant major and, shaking his head, walked away, into the orderly room.

"Move 'em out!" Sergeant Major Garrett ordered. "Sergeant

Dunn, have Private Hutchfield report to the company commander."

"I was about to ask permission anyway," I told Dunn.

"You got my permission to report to the mess sergeant after retreat for standing formation in a filthy uniform again," said Sergeant Dunn.

Without speaking to me, Sergeant Major Garrett flung his arm toward Lieutenant Glass's door. I knocked, was admitted, came to attention, rendered a smart military salute, said, "Private Hutchfield to see the company commander as ordered, surp."

"Private Hutchfield, as your company commander, I order you to report to the supply sergeant and secure a cartridge belt and wear it at all times while you are in the company area."

"Yes, sir."

I did it.

Then I returned to the orderly room, requested permission to see the company commander, was granted permission, knocked, was admitted, came to attention, rendered the proper military salute, intoned, "Private Hutchfield requests permission to speak to the company commander, surp."

Lieutenant Glass returned the salute. "Yes?" His tone was friendlier, as if he not only knew what it was like to be humiliated and had wanted me to suffer it, too, but that he now felt a little remorse for having been the agent of that humiliation, subject himself at any time to suffer it all over again.

"I request permission to visit the inspector general."

He was stricken. He couldn't refuse, any more than I could refuse to execute a direct order from my commanding officer—not without severe consequences. He didn't refuse. In a sputtering rage, he said, "Permission granted!"

"Which way do I go?"

"Find it yourself," he said, wanting to stomp me.

As I passed the sergeant major's desk, he grouched, "Join the company at school, Hutchfield. On the double."

"I have permission to visit the inspector general." I kept walking out the door, imagining the look on his face.

Not that I was eager to do it, not that I relished the irony. I was on my way to complain about the mistreatment of a trainee at the hands of a Negro company commander, a former ranger, who had worked harder than most to reach the goal he had set for himself, a goal not achieved with a lieutenant's bar.

The inspector general turned out to be a tall, lanky, bronzed, dark-haired Texan with deep-set eyes. He listened patiently to my story, including my complaint about the vicious circle of the uniform dirtied by KP, the impossibility of washing it before the next formation, having to go on KP again for wearing a filthy uniform.

He told me to hand over the new cartridge belt and dismissed me.

Walking back, wondering what the inspector general would do, I wasn't elated by my triumph.

A staff car full of brass passed me three minutes after I left the I.G.'s office. I wondered where they could be going in such a hurry.

When I reached the mess hall at the lower end of the company area, I could see across the parade ground through the screen door into the orderly room. Sergeant Major Garrett stood at rigid attention, a colonel, a major, and two captains glaring at him as the Texan chewed him out. With a swooshing movement, they all turned and burst through the side door and stalked up the path to the supply building, and as I reached my tent door, I saw the colonel toss the cartridge belt over the counter and rip a piece of paper in two and throw the pieces on the floor as Sergeant Marcos stood at attention, trying to decide whether to shit or go blind. And then the brass brigade turned and descended the steps and got into the staff car and roared away in a cloud of sandy dust. It was the cleanest, sharpest group movement I had ever seen. Swift, exhilarating. But I disliked it almost as much as I enjoyed it. And I was glad that Lieutenant Glass had not been in his office.

I waited a few moments, then, knots in my stomach, I knocked lightly at the orderly room door, afraid to wake the dead. Slumped in his swivel chair, Sergeant Major Garrett said, in a cold, neutral voice: "Wait in your tent until I send for you."

I sat on my bunk, reading Faulkner's A Fable, which I had bought out of my army pay—a limited, signed, numbered, case-bound edition.

Three hours later, just at chow time, Sergeant Brasbee's voice screeched out in the sun and sand. "Hutchfield! Re-port to the or-der-ly rooooom!"

I had almost reached the screen door when Lieutenant Glass walked out, in full uniform, looking terrific. A jeep was parked between the two pine trees just off the blacktop. Sergeant Keats was driving.

The lieutenant got into the backseat. He spoke quietly to Keats, who said to me, "Get in."

I started to get in beside Lieutenant Glass, because I knew the sergeant didn't want me sitting beside him, but Keats said, "Up front!"

So with the Negro officer in the backseat, we peeled out.

We passed the company marching in from school for noon chow. Stinnet, with his perpetual sleepy grin, was calling cadence: "Hut, tew, threet, hoor, Hutchfield keep in step!"

Lieutenant Glass and I had to wait, sitting side by side, a half hour before we were admitted to the inspector general's office.

Side by side, we rendered the proper military salute to the colonel from Texas who stood behind his desk, looking at tall, immaculate Lieutenant Glass and short, droopy Private Hutchfield. The colonel invited us to be seated side by side on the hard chairs.

The colonel informed Lieutenant Glass that Private Hutchfield had registered certain complaints and told him what they were. With no trace of sullenness, the lieutenant listened carefully. "What do you say to those charges, Lieutenant?"

"Sir, I intend to have Private Hutchfield court-martialed on six counts."

"You do that, Lieutenant Glass, and I will have *you* court-martialed on *seven* counts."

It was dramatic, it was impressive, it was *just*, but he was a Texan and Lieutenant Glass was an Arkansas "nigra," and I felt ashamed.

But the Texan didn't appear pleased with the situation, he did not gloat. Summing up, he spoke in a mild but firm tone: "Lieutenant Glass, I can see Private Hutchfield is not a good soldier, but he has certain rights nevertheless, and it is my duty as inspector general to protect those rights, just as I would protect yours."

I wanted to ask him whether he would protect Lieutenant Glass's rights back home in Texas, but then that would have made this a different story.

As I rode back with Lieutenant Glass, he seemed relaxed in the open jeep under the brutal South Carolina sun. Not at all tense or resentful. When he got out of the jeep, he walked easily into the orderly room. He hadn't won, but he had not contradicted, personally, Brasbee or Dunn or his other cadre.

I returned to my tent and opened *A Fable*. A few minutes later, Keats's face appeared at the screen, framed by his hands, a burst of sun behind him. "Let's go," he said, in a funereal voice.

I followed him to the jeep and got in beside him. As he peeled out of the sand and dust, I noticed, sticking out from under the seat between his legs, the blackish buckle of a cartridge belt.

When we passed the cutoff to the school, I wondered what the hell. Then swamp rose on both sides of the blacktop. Was he going to take me out into the boondocks and beat me to death with the cartridge belt? I remembered the scorching day at Camp Gordon in June when I was riding on a detail in a big truck driven by a young corporal, and he shut off the motor in the middle of the woods, and said, "Well, Hutchfield, right here's where they told me to beat your ass to a pulp." But he didn't. Instead, we rode wildly among the trees until he found a break in the fence and we hit a civilian rural road, and nearby lived his sister and we sat in her cool kitchen and drank lemonade and he told me how he went into the army when he was fourteen because he hated school.

I heard rifle fire. Then I remembered the company was supposed to go out to requalify and I was relieved until I recalled Keats saying he couldn't wait to get me on the rifle range.

I qualified again and then we all had to police up the brass.

"Hey, Hutchfield!" Keats yelled, behind me. I turned slowly, afraid his tone of sarcasm meant he would be aiming a rifle at me. The company, half of them on their knees in the tough, dry grass, half of them bent over at the waist, rose, turned expectantly, and looked at the new cartridge belt that dangled from Keats' upheld arm. "Found a stray cartridge belt. You can have it if you want it."

All the guys started patting their waists to see if they had dropped their belts. Then, relieved, they all laughed.

Lugging my helmet liner full of spent rounds, I walked back toward Keats, smiling. I liked him. I hoped he was going to hand it over in good grace. I wanted him to like me.

Clamping my brass-filled helmet liner between my knees, I took the cartridge belt from him, and as I snapped it on, he said, in a low voice, as quiet and even as Alan Ladd speaking to hired killer Wilson in *Shane*, "We're going to *get* your ass, Hutchfield. You made a fool out of your company commander and all the NCO's. You better look behind you, boy."

In the Bag

As he stepped off the 5:48, a bag and laughter shooshed down over his head.

"No!" A shoulder bump knocked him off balance, "Don't!" he fell, as if, for a moment, down an elevator shaft, he was caught, his feet were lifted, and he felt, through the soles of his shoes, a draw-string pulling tight. Picked up off the platform, he was carried, struggling, until his short gasps turned to nervous laughter, and he tried to relax into a joke.

Shoes, he couldn't hear how many, tramped in the hard snow. The laughter wasn't leaving the platform. Why was the crowd not following the joke to the end? Maybe they weren't part of the party. Only incidental spectators to its beginning. To scare him, his "abductors" must be stifling their own impulse to laugh.

To keep from spoiling their fun, he stopped laughing, pushed his mouth against his wool overcoat, snickered fitfully, and pretended to quake in fear. Weightless, he let himself be carried.

Had his wife and children been among the spectators and had they gone on ahead to the house? He imagined a sudden burst of raucous music. Let out of the bag, he'd blink at faces in bright light. Or was she helping them carry him? He couldn't distinguish the sex of hands.

They stopped. Awkwardly handled and turned, he tensed against falling. Let down on something soft, he was pushed and pulled, the bag rasping. He'd heard no doors open. They weren't in a hurry. Took time to set him upright. Hips shoved against him, on both sides. One door slammed, the other was pulled shut, quietly. Backseat. The ignition sparked. Except for its studded snow tires, the car ran smoothly, quietly, moved slowly. Maybe a limousine.

Where're they taking me?

The canvas smelled like the bag he'd used selling *Saturday Evening Posts* door to door, when he was nine, wearing corduroy knickers and a beanie clustered with Crackerjack prizes. A mailbag perhaps. But who would have access?

A lighter ignited, the smell of cigarette smoke put him at ease. Then it was gone, as if suddenly snuffed out.

He imagined some of the women he knew sewing scraps of colored cloth onto burlap or muslin, as at quilting bees he'd read about. Nice to step out of a bag with a bright Harlequin pattern. A woman's touch to fit the occasion?

But what was the occasion? His recent change of address showed he'd already achieved the promotion he'd worked so long to deserve. The dreary milestone birthday he'd always dreaded was months ahead in the spring. A reunion? The canvas smelled like a pup tent. His army buddies?

To work up saliva to speak, he clucked his tongue against the roof of his mouth. "Hey, you guys ever see action in Korea?" Faking a nervous voice made him more nervous. He'd lost track of his old army buddies.

A family reunion? "That you, Eric?" He hoped they didn't hear the catch in his throat. No, his family was scattered to the four corners.

Without an occasion, it would have to be impulse. A strange, a perverse impulse. His mouth was dry as a pocket.

What man or men did he know who were capable of such an audacious prank? Bagging a man as he stepped off the 5:48 local. He sorted through his small group of friends. The maze of his acquaintances. On the job. In the suburbs. In the church. Plenty of guys in the army, but none he'd known well enough. A few kids in the neighborhood where he grew up, in the public schools, a few in his college fraternity. Something his brother would dream up? Not likely. His sister? Certainly not. He wished a little light from somewhere would filter into the bag.

Nobody spoke. Two in the back. The driver made three. Perhaps a fourth and fifth up front. *The more the merrier.*

"Okay, what's going on, fellas?" In the bag, the voice was not his own.

They seemed to be holding their breath, enforcing a resolute silence. The car swayed gently, seemed to climb a slope. The timbre of traffic noise made him see the freeway. None between the station and his house. He'd moved from one small town to another to avoid stalled homebound traffic. The freeway was a scare tactic. Being in the bag and the darkness magnified his heartbeat.

To provoke a response, he said, "Boy, you guys really surprised me back there . . . . I was never so unprepared for a practical joke in my life . . . . Clever, too. Anybody can sneak a hot foot or rig a bucket of water over a door . . . . Say, who was it hit on the idea?" He listened for suppressed snickers. The silence made him more aware of his cold feet. "Come on, don't be bashful. Take credit."

A bit of lint tickled his nose. He'd never seen a laundry bag big enough to encase a man. A man in an overcoat. He tried to sneeze. The car was heating up. The canvas smelled like a gymnasium. He wished he could get out of the overcoat. Be comfortable. Enjoy the joke. But maybe his enjoyment was not one of the features. Some jokes were constructed unfairly that way. Everything rigged for the delight of the perpetrators alone.

How did he get off on this tangent? He was as good a sport as any man he knew. But in the fraternity, if the victim wasn't terrified, the gag was no fun for the tricksters. Though he'd always lacked imagination, he'd devised a few terrors himself. In on the practical jokes in the barracks, too. And at the office. Less and less an instigator, but always a participant. Revenge? No, surely not. Never anything serious. Good clean fun.

He heard sniffling, muffled perhaps by a handkerchief, and the bag.

Framed in the stairwell of the train, he always felt shy, as if when his wife's searching eyes found him, others would stare. So he hadn't been looking for her among the parked cars and station wagons, but had noticed below the steps a tarred pipe cleaner, then, as his toe touched the platform, heard wind popping in a sail, looked up as the flapping canvas swooped down, the butt of a palm gripping the edge, a dull flash of sky. The shoosh of instant laughter and swift canvas.

Someone tried to blow his nose without being heard.

His wife would worry. His children would be watching her, absorbing the atmosphere of anxiety her expressions, intonations, gestures, movements would conjure up. Their whimpering would make her, like the woman in the headache commercial, snap at them.

"Just to put my mind at ease, is my wife in on this? No sense in worrying *her*."

But why would she worry? Had she been ignorant of the scheme, seeing him appear in the stairwell, watching them slip the bag over his head, pull the drawstring tight over his feet, she would have screamed at the sight. But maybe they diverted her attention. Or stopped her on the way to the station. Before she left, captive now in the house.

Where are you taking me? He was afraid he was about to breathe up all the oxygen.

A little fearful of the reaction he might provoke, but wanting a clearer expression of the nature of his relationship with the perpetrators, he struggled, heaved forward, the canvas rough against his cheek, the hips, wedged against his, did not budge. He bumped against rigid shoulders. As if to retract his gesture of defiance, he sat still, listening to the snow tires.

He was almost certain he heard taxi horns. The sound of cars rushing by seemed to come through closed windows. A sudden stop made him lurch forward, but he was still wedged between shoulders and hips.

Inside the overcoat, he perspired profusely. But his feet were still cold. He sneezed, a soggy detonation that made his ears ring numbly.

The car was not moving. Listening for every nuance of sound, sensitive to every movement, he'd missed the gentle braking. But he heard the doors open: three, maybe four, all at once. Efficient.

When the shoulders and hips released him, he tipped forward, tried to balance himself on the edge of the seat. Then they pushed him over, not viciously, onto his side. Pulled by his ankles, out.

The freezing air stabbed through the canvas, the overcoat. He was lifted, carried, afraid they'd drop him. From the car door, brief transit inside somewhere. Hearing no door close behind. Some kind of fraternal order? Through the back door into a restaurant where his wife and children and friends and acquaintances and relatives awaited his arrival? Maybe it was his birthday after all. The ceremonious opening of the harlequin bag. His eyes blinking at candles ablaze in an enormous room. Sudden laughter at the startled expression on his face, then singing, as the soles of his feet, asleep, tingled.

His buttocks touching the floor triggered a convulsion. He was there, where they wanted him to be.

He felt alone. Abandoned, in the dark of the bag, in the dark of a building. Smothered, he fought to reach the mouth of the bag. Tried to scream but could not. Violent twisting, turning brought his head up against the tied end of the bag.

He forced his finger into the bag's mouth, the tight pleats loosened, and a blessing of air and light slowly blossomed in the expanding hole.

Two sets of hands were pulling the bag open. A woman's long red fingernails, a gleaming gold ring. Knuckles rubbed the back of his head. In the glaring light, the woman stepped back, her eyes enormous, mouth open in shock. He sucked in air. The odor of perfume, rouge, and powder, as if heated by the lights.

An unbuttoned collar, the bag hung around his neck. He squatted in the living room of a very elegant house. Double doors. Paintings in elaborate frames. A grand piano, cut flowers lying in a basket on the closed lid. Decor of an earlier century.

The woman's terrified expression was heavily rouged. She wore dangling earrings. The red fingernails touched in a prayerful position. Now she looked desperately over his head.

Turning, he looked up into painfully bright lights at the silhouette of a man. Beyond the bank of lights, darkness. Slowly, the man's black tie took on definition against his white shirt front. He wore tie and tails. Was he a magician? Am I a rabbit coming out of a sack? About to laugh, he sensed he must not. The way he'd seen a photograph being developed in a movie, a man's face slowly became more distinct: an expression of ripe panic.

He'd known intuitively that their terror was not a pretense. The joke was not on him alone then, but on two equally surprised actors in the middle of a play.

At his back, he sensed the audience, beyond the lights, out there in the darkness. He did not want to look out there. As if he were hanging by a root off a cliff, a look down might inspire an impulsive release.

The two actors were looking to each other for help, but he sensed the audience accepting these events as an integral part of the play.

In the next pure, incandescent moment, he winked at the woman, and passed the instant when he could have shot up out of the bag and run out of the room, avoiding a situation perilously locked in panic. With that wink, he committed himself to helping the woman and the man salvage a situation into which the totally unexpected had intruded.

His wink lessened the strain in her face. She was relying upon him, too, for help. He sensed that the help she needed was absolute silence and immobility. The man's strategy, too, was to freeze.

The woman and the room in which she stood and now began to move, tentatively, were faintly familiar. Still, his heart beat faster, his mouth got dryer.

As the woman's face began to show that she was recovering from the shock of seeing his head emerge from the bag, he felt a little proud of himself for not dashing off in his own panic.

But now the woman's face showed a new emotion. Hatred. Had she returned to the script? No, she was looking directly into his eyes, as if she regarded him as a conspirator in a joke played upon her and her fellow actor by other members of the cast, or perhaps the crew.

"My dear Archer," she said, over his head, gaining control with each careful inhalation of breath, each syllable she uttered, "I should, of course, scold you severely for leading me to expect an empty bag. All that talk was designed merely to set me up, wasn't it?"

"I must, yes, Madam, I must confess," said Archer, becoming, perhaps, a butler, "to having deliberately, as you say, although I rather dislike the phrase, 'set you up'."

With a flourish, Madam showed Archer her back and did a slow turn about the room. He admired the grace and speed with which she mastered her personal emotions and quite adroitly slipped into an improvised escape from the disruptive situation into which she had been thrust.

Was she a star he had failed, overwhelmed by his own fear and nervousness, to recognize, and was Archer's a minor role?

His back to the audience, he felt safer in the bag than outside, walking about the room, where he'd have to make each movement mean something in a play, the plot of which he was ignorant.

On his knees in the bag, his overcoat doubling the heat under the lights, he watched them, wondering, *If they draw me into whatever they're improvising, what note must I strike—a comic or a tragic?* Madam's own tone was not a safe cue. The demand that was being made upon his imagination and perhaps some hidden talent for performance excited and frightened him.

"What am I to do now, Madam?"

Now it was at Archer that Madam shot a look of hatred. Was she turning the action in another direction with Archer's help, or was she reproaching him as an actor for a lack of invention, for shifting the entire burden of ingenuity upon her?

He wanted to risk speaking or coming out of the bag to rescue both Madam and Archer. But the realization, based on his own experience out there, that one had an even greater obligation to the audience at his back than to the actors, struck him dumb again, and he froze, certain he'd say the wrong thing, make the wrong move, and reduce the situation to its original chaos.

"*Do? Do?*" She asked, haughtily, making fat pauses. "My dear Archer, it was you who routed me out at this ungodly hour to receive a bag full of trash delivered by two surly men from god knows where."

"But, Madam, they insisted," said Archer, reaching, slowly, for words. "And they assured me that it would prove vitally important to you. A matter, in fact, of life or death."

"And as you can see, the bag is not at all empty, not full of old newspapers or whatever it was you told me. In fact, sticking out of it, for all the world to see, is the head of—of—of a deaf mute."

He winced, afraid she'd blown it. For how could the character she played *know* that this stranger in the bag was a deaf mute?

But no murmur of disbelief came from the audience. In a rush of awe and love, he imagined that the audience had known from the moment his head burst through the mouth of the sack that a mistake or a joke had happened, and instinctively, as a single body and mind, had collaborated with the actors and the intruder to achieve possibilities only fear and hope could pose. They trusted the star to cover her move later. Serving both, he was neither actor nor audience.

How clever of her, after all, to inform the audience that they were not to expect the man squatting in the bag to speak. Even if she could not know whether he were an actor himself, or, if an actor, a good or a mediocre one, she'd covered all possibilities with that brilliant stroke of improvisation.

But he began to resent her solution. He'd impulsively chosen to risk helping the woman and the man save the situation, triumph over the joke, or the accident. He wanted to jump out of the bag and overwhelm the actress with a feat of dumb show.

But that, he realized, was an overreaching ambition for a man with perhaps only minutes to go before the professionals found a way to get rid of him or the script required the curtain to fall. Within his natural limitations, he'd do what he could to earn the actors' gratitude, simultaneously earning a sense of achievement in the eyes of the audience at his back. His mouth dry as the canvas bag, his heart beat almost comically hard and fast.

The audience was too quiet for a comedy. Or were they hushed for a famous line the reviewers had alerted them to expect at this point?

"Shall I remove him, Madam?"

Archer came into view, to the left. Madam moved up from the piano. Had the bit player innocently upstaged the star? His wife sometimes pointed out such things.

No wonder Madam looked familiar. And the room. He'd seen both before. With his wife. A long-running Broadway hit. A light mystery comedy. Not a musical, thank God. He could neither sing nor dance, nor, as his high school drama coach had gently told him, act.

The play, he remembered, called for the delivery of a grimy bag, expected, after much talk designed to set up not just Madam but the audience as well, to be stuffed with waste paper. To everyone's shock and surprise, the bag was to have contained a corpse.

And this joke, so reckless as to be almost certainly some kind of revenge upon the star, delivered instead, a living nonactor.

He still couldn't recall the star's name, but he recognized the butler now, from bit parts in many other plays he'd seen with his wife. Too many of them boring flops. Or boring hits. He'd forgotten how this one turned out. A long Friday at the office, a few martinis, a steak. It was a joke among the men at his church, "Who's slept through the most third acts?"

The double doors flung open and a boy and girl of about seven and nine came skipping and hopping into the room. "Mother, may we see, may we see what those men delivered?"

"Mother" became a tower of matchsticks, about to lean. No one had thought to head off the kids. He felt sorry for her. She didn't deserve this blow.

Seeing him alive in the bag, the children stopped, waving their arms for balance, as if tottering on the edge of a high wall. That same pathetic look of panic. They'd often played this scene as rehearsed. Rushing to the bag in a thrilling fit of giggles, they, he remembered, were supposed to discover the corpse, then flee, screaming. They looked desperately to the two grownups, the star and the bit player.

His back still to the audience, conjuring from memory the hideous face he used to make to scare his little sister on dark nights walking home from the movies, he suddenly shot up out of the bag. The boy and the girl ran screaming from the room.

The audience's nervous laughter made him want to turn and bow to it, but he knew that that would blow the moment.

Then he realized he'd created a dilemma: once they got him out of the room and managed a way to bring a second bag in, who would discover the corpse the plot demanded?

As the star moved toward him, he saw her mind working, and felt a rising exhilaration that tickled his throat. Suddenly, pointing at him, she shrieked, "Look! Look, Archer! A dagger!"

Archer came into view, and, relieved by her solution, pretended that what he saw horrified him.

Remembering that the children's discovery of the corpse ended act one, he clutched his stomach and, being careful to fall so that the audience could not see that no dagger stuck out of his body, sank to the floor, his feet still inside the bag.

"Quick, Archer! Help me!"

He heard the star and the bit player rush toward him. They lifted his body, that he let sag dead-weight, and braced it up with their own bodies. Feeling the canvas shoosh up over his body again, he felt the keenest euphoria he'd ever known.

Proud of the star and the bit player and of the children and of himself, he was eager to hear the creak of the pulleys as the curtain came down, the hail of applause, and to receive the adulation of the grateful actors when he told them that he, no actor at all, had been an unknowing participant in the trick, and hoped they would call him from the wings to take a bow with them for repeated curtain calls.

As the canvas flapped at his ears, coming up around his head, and he felt their hands fumbling for the drawstrings, gagging rose in his throat, a smothery suction at his nose and mouth, and he risked detection by the audience, lifting his head to watch the neck of the bag close, the light iris out.

Lindbergh's Rival

I'm standing in the bright sun, in front of the abandoned neighborhood theater in my hometown, Cherokee, telling my little boy about the movies I used to see there—*The Sea Hawk*, *The Curse of the Cat People*, *Stagecoach*, *Trail of the Lonesome Pine*, *Public Enemy*, *Flying Tigers*—when an image comes to me somehow connected with this neighborhood or those old movies, something I think really happened: a man is bent over, his back to me, and he's building an airplane in his basement—a real fullscale airplane. If I ever saw him with my own eyes, I don't remember. Maybe my dad told me about it.

"Come on," I say to my boy, "let's walk the way I used to go when I was a kid coming home from the Rialto," and we cross the most dangerous intersection in Cherokee.

We stop on the bridge and I toss rocks and old Popsicle sticks over the railing into the dark green water. "This is where I used to throw rocks and stuff."

"You're still doing it." He just stands there in his new outfit, fancy boots planted wide apart, his palms resting on the handles of the six-shooters, looking at me from under the brim of the big red cowboy hat that shades his face.

He follows me down the bank, and we walk along until we come to the WPA ditch that empties into the creek, and I say, "Now, if we follow this ditch, we'll come out right where I used to live."

He follows me, but I know he misses his mama. Maybe he's figured out why this is the first trip we've ever taken without her. And maybe he senses what *she's* probably guessed by now—that this trip to Cherokee is to give him something to remember me by after I leave.

The ditch runs through the middle of a field that's still wild with kudzu vines and honeysuckle, blackberry vines and horsechestnut trees leaning over both sides of it, and I still want to play like we're fighting through a jungle, and I'm still just as scared of snakes as I ever was. We dash through, my boy and I, and finally come out safe at the little wooden bridge where I used to sit and dangle my legs and spit into the rainwater boiling along beneath my feet.

"Hey, there's where old Jack Carmichael lived," I say to my boy. "I used to stick my ear down in the warm water in the bottom of his daddy's rowboat after a rain and listen to the sound of the sea." The boat no longer sits in the side yard, between the clothesline and the jungle.

Where our house used to be, there's only a red clay field covered with dewberry vines, shriveling in the August heat. Since we moved out twenty-some years ago, it burned two or three times, and the last time I saw it, fire had gutted it, but the frame still stood, and I craved to buy it then, fix it up, and stay there whenever I came back to Cherokee to visit my folks.

I tell my boy that I used to bury little dead kitties in that red clay bank. "Stick 'em in fruit jars full of flowers." But I don't tell him what my mother told me a few years before—that I was born at home and that my daddy buried my afterbirth in that bank.

I say to my boy, "Let's jump in the ditch again and follow it to my old schoolhouse."

As we turn the corner of the ditch where it makes a sharp jog around a yellow house, I remember the two little girls who used to come to the back of the yard and look over the fence—still covered with honeysuckle vines—and I'd show them my "dodopeepeesoso." One was a cute little blonde girl that I lost track of when we moved away, and the other was a dark, slightly cross-eyed girl named Jewel Harper, a nasty, dirty girl, the other kids thought, but I remember a strange, off-center beauty that haunts me in dreams.

We're about to walk on, when I see a short, trim woman in lemon shorts and lavender halter, pushing an old-fashioned lawnmower.

She must be about fifty, but she's sort of cute, attractive, and I remember I used to see her in downtown Cherokee after I moved away from Davanna Street—cashier in a drugstore, I think—and it hits me she's the mother of a little curly-blackhaired kid I've been remembering over the years. He had the shiniest toys during those late Depression years, and he wasn't allowed to play with me. Nothing big was made of it; I just understood I wasn't supposed to go into his yard. With his white house, that had green shutters, his daddy's car, and his own little red car parked on his neat little front porch, he always stood for something—better.

His mother's looking at us. So I wave. She looks at me, stops mowing, waves back, yells, "Aren't you Irene Hutchfield's little boy?"

I say, "Yes, ma'am."

So she starts asking about me and my parents and I tell her a few lies.

"I'm living in Ohio now," I tell her, and that much is true. "We're just passing through. Little trip to Texas—promised to show my boy the Alamo."

She says, "Well, come on up out of that ditch and have some lemonade with me. Don't you know it's hot?"

I say, "Let's go, Byron," he says, "Naw, I wanna run in this ditch," so I say, "Okay, but be careful, hear? Don't go too far. Your mama'd kill me if you got lost."

I walk behind the lady through the cut grass, and we pass this wide garage door—closed—and it's then I remember the image that came to me in front of the Rialto: that man, building a real airplane in his garage. And I'm thinking, well, now that's got to be too weird to have been actual. So I didn't ask her about it. What if it turned out to be crazy? But there's that strange garage, set right under the house, the driveway swooping around to the side. Even back then I thought it was odd, a garage situated like that, under the house, with stone walls. I never saw another garage like that in all of Cherokee.

So we go up the steep back steps and into her kitchen, and she squeezes the lemons and we drink lemonade and talk about the old times.

She says, "It's hard on a woman like me not to have a husband. I'm no spring chicken, but it's hard not to have a man around."

I say, "Well, what happened to your husband?"

She says, "Don't you remember? He was killed overseas."

I say, "I don't think I ever knew that."

She says, "That's right, you all had moved to Sevier Street."

And I say—all of a sudden, I realize who he was—I say, "That little red and green truck! Didn't he used to deliver for Perfecto Cleaners?"

"Sure did," she says.

"I never really saw much of him when we lived across the street, but after we moved, every time he stopped for some cleaning, my mama'd say, 'Honey, you remember him, don't you?' and I'd say, 'Yeah,' but I never was sure. My momma always said he looked like Robert Taylor. Had a thin moustache, and slim?"

And she says, "That's right," with this look on her face like she knows just what that meant: that my mother, along with all the other women on his route, thought her husband looked like Robert Taylor, just like William Bonnie himself in *Billy the Kid* that time it played the Rialto, black outfit, even a black leather jacket. "He was a very handsome man," she says, "and don't think it isn't rough after having a man like that in the house . . ."

Seems to me she's getting kind of sexy, so I keep waiting for her to give a more obvious signal.

I recall again how she never let me play with her son, never let him out of his yard. But I used to see him later, at a distance, in junior high and senior high. And one time, he was the manager of a basketball team my girl played on, and they posed for a picture for the Cherokee *Sentinel*, and he asked me to stand on one side to balance the picture and play like I was a manager, too. I felt good about that since he was even shorter than I was. I ask his mother about him, and she says, "He's married, doing fine, got him a nice wife, good job, this nice, big new car, and the cutest little boy you ever laid eyes on." I picture him a tiny kid still, like a Charlie McCarthy doll in a tuxedo, driving around Cherokee in a Buick.

"Listen," I say, because how often do you get a chance to fit your memory to the facts—"can I ask you a question?"

She says, "Go ahead."

I say, "Was your husband building an airplane down there in your garage?"

And she says, "Yes." She says, "He didn't tell anybody about it, it was sort of a secret, but I reckon people found out about it, though, and then forgot it." She says, "But I guess you haven't."

I say, "No, it stuck in my mind."

So she tells me how it happened.

It was the same year that Lindbergh flew to Paris. And she and her husband were on their honeymoon in New York when Lindbergh returned. "I was in love with the Lone Eagle, and it showed, but he didn't say anything, he just listened to me go on and on about the Lone Eagle, the Lone Eagle, the Lone Eagle, and bought me every newspaper and magazine and souvenir I craved.

"Then soon as we moved into this house—fact, I think he picked it for that garage—well, we moved from an apartment across town—why, he commenced to build that thing. But he wasn't in any great hurry about it, and he had to provide for his family. So he took this job delivering for Perfecto. But in his spare time, why, he would work on that airplane. You know, the way a man would work on any kind of hobby. A little bit more, I guess . . ." And she says, "I went along with it."

She filled our glasses with lemonade again and fanned her breasts with a damp dish cloth. "I used to lie awake picturing him in the cockpit of a silver plane, landing in Paris or Casablanca. What he was going to do, he was going to start from New York, fly all the way around the world, come all the way back, go Lindbergh one better. I could see him so plain, that handsome man, pushing back his goggles, his white silk scarf fluttering, getting out of the cockpit, his moustache— Yeah, he looked like Robert Taylor, all right.

"I never discouraged him. Got hard on me sometimes, but . . . And then he was drafted into the army in the fall of 19-and-42, and they buried him in France. I left him over there. I couldn't bear to disturb his body."

I was certain she was going to cry, but she didn't.

So we talked a while longer, and then I said, "Well, better see how my boy's doing."

I started to go, but she says, "Don't you want to *see* it?"

I say, "You mean you still *got* it?"

She says, "Come on."

So she opens a door in the kitchen, and the basement's pitch dark. And she says, "Listen, I better take your hand, because the light won't work from up here." Says, "I can feel around in the dark and I know exactly where the cord hangs."

And so, I think, here it comes, and I can smell her—pushing that lawnmower in the hot sun. And I think, well, *you* know, I'll just see what happens, and I follow her down. All of a sudden, a light comes on, and there it is.

And it looks—I don't know the first thing about airplanes—but it just looks all—in every conceivable way—wrong.

"Of course," she says, "it's not finished yet . . ."

The fuselage is made of two or three different kinds of metal, beaten into shape with a hammer, and some patches of it are painted, some are rusted, the engine and propeller are mounted in what looks like an oversized soapbox racer, the wings are covered with canvas, and one scrap at the tip has Cherokee *Sentinel* stenciled on it—the kind of satchel I used when I carried papers—bicycle wheels are the landing gear, and the rudder is a Coca-Cola sign worked into shape.

So we look at it in the 40-watt light, and I say, "Well, I bet this really tickled your little boy when his daddy was building it!" I was about to ask her to let *my* boy come sit in the cockpit a while.

She says, "Well, he wouldn't let him touch it, wouldn't let *me* touch it, wouldn't let anybody touch or go near it. He'd never say, 'Come, look what I did today.' But he didn't mind us seeing how he was coming along. He'd let us stand at the top of the stairs and look down. Naturally, my little boy loved to look. Just thrilled him to pieces.

"So when we got word he was killed, it seemed to me that the most natural thing in the world would be to come down here and look at the airplane—give my son a way to, *you* know, remember his daddy. Hadn't *seen* him in about two years. Sure, there were these handsome pictures of him all over the house, but still, here was something from father to son. So we came down here, and he didn't say anything. Then I say, 'Would you like to sit in the cockpit?'

"He said, 'No!' And that really hurt me, you know? I thought, 'Well, my God! Here you've got some way of feeling for your father, and—!'

"So, I left him down there, shut the door, locked it. Well, he screamed and he screamed *and* he screamed—you all had moved to Sevier Street by then—till I felt *so* bad, I opened the door, and just begged that pitiful thing to forgive me.

"Well, I suppose he did. He comes to see his mother every weekend, mostly, with his wife and little Bobby. But he never comes down here, and I don't suppose I blame him.

"Of course, to *me*, it's a familiar thing, you know? I get my lawn-mower out of here and—*you* know, things like that."

I say, "Well, guess I better see how my little boy is." I look through one of the grimy panes in the garage door. "I don't see his red hat sticking up above the ditch."

"Want to go out this way?" she says, and then she heaves up the garage door, one of those pull-up jobs on pulleys, and the sunlight bursts in on the windshield of the thing. All of a sudden, it looks pretty good—not such a mistake—that terrific light on the propeller. You can see it has a fine grade of wood, and all the polishing it's had. But you can see something else—the wingspread is too wide to get the plane through the door. Much too wide. And the walls are made of field stone.

When I point this out to her—thinking she's just forgotten to mention it to me—she acts like she doesn't hear.

"Can I do anything for you?" I say.

She says, "No, just go on. I'm glad you came by . . ."

So I cross the fresh-cut grass and look up and down the ditch. I don't see my boy anywhere. I think, my God! I can't believe he's gone back to the creek! "Frankly, I just don't think you're responsible enough," my wife told me when we were arguing about this trip.

No, he probably kept going along the ditch the way we were headed—running. He loves a free run like that. I run on down the ditch, toward my old grammar school, past some sprawly, smooth gray rocks that lie in the green grass among vines. They look cool. I've forgotten them all these years. I come to the end of the ditch, and I look up and down the street. No sign. I face it—he's at the creek! But then I hear chains creaking and turn and there he is, swinging in the backyard with some little boys.

He yells, "Where you been?"

All I ever tell him is, "Talking to that lady, and drinking lemonade."

On Target

In one of the pine-floored tents on Tank Hill, Frank sat on the edge of his bunk, the coal smoke making tears streak his face.

From the bunk above, bare feet long as Frank's forearm hung down without the slightest muscle twitch. Mixed with the coal smoke and the swelling gas in Frank's stomach from the slop he had been too hungry to refuse after a solid day of tests (that might have made him eligible for Officer's Training School if he hadn't dropped out of high school), the smell of the feet almost knocked him out. So he supposed the letter to Rachel would sound as though it came from a loony bin. By the 40-watt bulbs, they all looked, their heads sticking up out of the coal haze, like men and boys in solitary confinement.

The fellow up above wore regular farmer's overalls, bib and straps, that brought the smell of hogs with them. Somebody must have given him the glossy red shirt with the scrawly design for a going-away present, expecting him, perhaps, never to return. Over the overalls and the shirt, he wore a navy surplus blue-black jacket.

The stitches on his brown leather helmet showed where the goggles used to be. The strap was buckled tight under his chin, puffing out his cheeks. The blond sheep's lining spilling out at the hairline was the same color as the blade of hair that curved between his brows. His eyes, brown as the richest loam, stared. Around his soft mouth was a blond beard too thin and short to shave.

He had not been on the bus that brought Frank down from Logan, West Virginia. He had been there already on the top bunk, alone in the tent, when Frank followed the others in. A sergeant had turned Frank around and given him a little shove toward the bunk and he'd stumbled over the guy's shoes.

His hands, huge like his feet, cupped in his lap, he perched on the cot, the mattress still rolled, the springs bare, as Frank finished his letter. And he was staring straight ahead when the speaker outside ordered "lights out," and someone snapping off the light broke the cord.

Frank, who had lied about his age to get in the army so he could support his mother and his sixteen-year-old wife, lay on the bottom bunk, listening to the pine tree hovering over the tent, imagining the silver-painted water tank catching the moonlight outside. Thinking of Rachel, he fell asleep with an erection.

The next morning, the farm boy was gone, but the smell stuck around.

That evening after chow, they were issued their uniforms and wore them back. Entering the tent, Frank almost stumbled into a guy who was bent over splattering his new trousers with what his stomach rejected.

At the first glint of light the next morning, the men were spread out the length of several blocks and told to move between some deserted barracks. "I don't want to see nothing but buttholes and elbows," said the corporal behind them. The buttocks and elbows that moved directly in front of Frank straightened up, and the corporal ran up to the guy and turned him around. It was the farm boy with the rank bare feet. Stuffing cigarette butts into the shirt pocket of his uniform, the boy said, "I thought I'd roll me a few."

The white name tag stitched above his breast pocket was blank. But when Frank saw him next, in the basic training company to which he was assigned a few days later, the boy's name tag read ROOKS, printed freehand with ink that ran.

Thanks to something called the "buddy system," Frank got stuck to Rooks—the guy with the shoes that pinched so hard he often cried, and hair like on a Shirley Temple doll.

> . . . I hoped when they assigned us to companies, I'd
> lose my buddy. The trouble is, Rachel, *I'm* not much

better. Seems like I don't know how to shine a damn shoe
or make a damn bed or mop a damn floor or keep the hell
in step.

Don't tell Momma and them. In a few months I'll be
what I set out to be, but meantime I'm what is known as
a—well, I reckon "screw-up" will do.

And it don't help to have the platoon sergeant com-
pare me with this dumb-bunny Rooks. "Look at Rooks,"
he'll say. "How hard you have to *try* to look as neat as
him?" I look at him. And I look at me, and I don't see
we're so much alike we *both* have to ride the range—like
we did tonight. What they make you do is clean out
these big coal stoves as clean as if the General was going
to eat breakfast on one. So when you're through at
twelve, after marching all day, you have to clean your
rifle in the shower room while everybody's asleep, and
Rooks keeps banging his "piece"—they call it—against
the sink and they yell at *us*, and *me* not making sound
one.

Rooks is smart. He doesn't really spend time cleaning
his rifle. He sticks it in the sink, lets the hot water run
on it for an hour, and he goes and sits on one of the
eleven barefaced commodes across from the bowls and
mirror and falls asleep sitting straight up, and when I
look around at him the next time, he's tipped over side-
wise, his cheek resting on the roll of toilet paper screwed
to the wall, his boots on the damp concrete like a pair
dropped by a hunter that the dogs took one sniff of and
left.

. . . I do everything they tell me to do, I don't even
have to hold myself in from telling them off. Because I
want to make squad leader.

But seems like they got it in for me. Maybe they see
I'm trying too hard. But I don't see why that puts me
with Rooks. Because he doesn't try or not try, he's just
there, and sometimes the move he makes gets him by
and sometimes, if he gives the wrong answer or makes
the wrong move, like lashing somebody cross the head

with his M1 while doing an about-face at the wrong signal, Sergeant Allen starts him trotting around the company area with his rifle over his head till he drops. And
then he comes right back and stands at ease the wrong
way, and turns up at the grease pit outside the messhall
just as I'm getting down on my stomach to skim the
scum off the top.

What did *I* do? Fell the hell asleep during *the naming
of parts*—this Mickey Mouse class where we have to learn
what an M1 is made up of.

Why did I fall asleep? Because I didn't get done cleaning my blamed rifle and squaring my equipment away
for inspection till two o'clock, and then they jerked us
out at five and we didn't get formed up on the parade
ground quick enough to suit Sergeant Allen, so he run us
back in. "Fall out!" and we did, but not fast enough.
"Fall out!" and then he marched us while the other platoons ate up all the chow.

. . . Well, Rachel, things are getting a little better
now. An officer happened to catch me lettering my name
on my footlocker without a stencil and he asked me if I
would report to him tomorrow morning. First time anybody's *asked* me to do something in this army.

. . . It turns out, he wanted me to paint a blue band
with a white border on about eighty helmet liners for the
cadre who train us. So that's what I did today while the
rest were out on the rifle range in knee-knocking cold.

At about one o'clock, a jeep pulls up outside this
empty barracks where they had me painting, and took
me way out down the highway and deep into the woods
at this place where they got about thirty targets and he
said he had orders to rush me through. The lieutenant
was up in a tower, giving instructions. The other guys
standing out in that freezing November wind didn't like
the sight of me going ahead. There I was up ahead of
them, moving from one yardage point to another, right
in the middle of the range, all the other targets still on

both sides, and mine working up and down like crazy.

And I do mean crazy, honey, because the lieutenant kept screaming at whoever was in the pit working the target. He put the wrong color markers in the wrong holes every time, till I wasn't sure what I was doing.

Allen was my instructor, and he kept giving me a hard time, and then he said I'd better paint him a special helmet for dress parade, one with an eagle on it so real he'd be afraid to touch it for fear he'd get bit. Something about the way he said it made me feel he likes me. Looking back, I saw the rest of the company just diddling around, waiting for *this* regimental favorite to get done boloing. That's what you are if you don't make the minimum score. A bolo. And that's what I did. Boloed.

And when I started back down the field toward them, Allen behind me like I was something out of the stockade that had to walk twenty paces ahead of the man with the carbine, they all started laughing and pointing— their fingers, I mean. This one guy closest to me, I almost reached out and stroked his chin with the butt of my M1, but I controlled it.

Tonight, while we were scrubbing down the messhall (nobody told me what I did wrong today), Rooks told me he was sure tired. "What from?" I asked, to be nice. "Pulling and jerking at them worrisome targets," he said, and I poured a bucket of dirty mop water right over his head. He shook himself like a dog, slinging a few drops on me, and whimpered a little and wiped it out of his hair, then went back to scrubbing.

I'm sorry I did it, so when he falls asleep on that commode, I'm gonna shine his boots up for him, and maybe they won't put him on KP again for *that*. Something else for sure, but not *that*.

. . . I wish Momma wouldn't keep asking when I'm going to make PFC. She doesn't seem to realize that you don't make *any*thing till you get out of basic and get assigned to some permanent job. The way things look, they're going to ship me to Vietnam.

That's okay by me. A bunch of guys in the training cycle that's just finishing in the company down the street says you see a lot of action. Your uniform is green and you blend with the landscape.

. . . Well, I don't have much more to go now. If I can just get through it all, with this extra stuff they make me do—those helmet liners, and now all kinds of lettering around the company area and even over at regimental. Just because I was forced into that damn mechanical drawing course in the tenth grade. It hasn't done me any good, after all. Just more bitterness than ever. The guys hate my guts even though I hardly talk to them. They think calling Rooks my sweetheart tees me off, but it just makes me want to try harder to show them up.

But Allen is nicer to me now and doesn't look so hard for ways to put me on KP or make me do push-ups. I brought that eagle to him in his room last night, and he had on just his shorts from coming out of the shower, but he put the helmet on and went down the hall to Corporal Faw's room and woke him up and made him look at it.

And this morning, he woke us all up wearing it. Swaggered around like he was a bald eagle himself. And for my part, I'd swear he was. It made me feel good to know that I had something to do with the act he put on.

. . . We had general inspection today. The bird colonels came around and looked at every man in the company.

A major that looked like Errol Flynn was with them. He kept picking up the bores of the M1's (a piece of our pieces) and going over to the window and looking up at the sun through the bores.

In the same casual way, he came to Rooks's and looked up his, but the quiet, slow way he said, "Good God," behind my back made the shaved hairs prickle on my neck and my ears burn. "Sergeant," he said to Allen, "make this man sign a statement of charges for this ri-

fle—it's ruined. If he had fired it, it would have blown
his face off. I'd like to *look* at that face."

He stepped around and looked at Rooks and yelled at
him to render the proper salute, and Rooks rendered
something that made him say, "Good God," again, and
then he started talking to Rooks. But what Rooks said,
which I didn't get, did something deep to him, because
when he sidestepped over to me and I snapped to and
rendered the proper salute and caught a glimpse of his
face before I turned to stone, he looked like Errol Flynn
turned seventy. "That's more like it," he said, weakly, to
my salute. Then he stepped back to Rooks and backed off
from him several separate times and shook his head and
said to the colonel, "Sir, wouldn't you say to even court-
martial something like that would be a crime?"

"On our part," said the colonel, nodding, like a big
wholesaler looking at a crop he'd counted on buying but
that had blighted.

Then the major looked at *my* rifle and said to Allen,
"Sergeant, it might be a good idea if you sort of assigned
this man to watch over Rooks. Who's the squad leader?"

"Rankin, sir."

He went down the line and the tone of his voice talking to Rankin wasn't too good.

As they passed by me, leaving the barracks, I heard
the colonel say, "Sergeant, you better hold that helmet
down with both hands. Looks to me like that thing's got
some eggs to get back to." They all laughed, good buddies like, and Sergeant's face turned pink with pleasure.

. . . You know what that Rooks is going around telling everybody? He's going around telling everybody that
his brother stood up on the machine-gun range and was
killed and that he's going to do the same thing. Bright
and early in the damned morning. These guys think
that's the funniest thing they ever heard, but Allen,
who's been in Korea and seen a few, called me in and told
me to keep an eye on Rooks tomorrow. So I reckon he'll
be crawling along beside me.

. . . Dear Rachel, Rooks stood up.

I had my face down on the hard dirt and gravel, trying to get my breath to push forward again, when somebody screamed. When I turned my head sideways, there was Rooks like a giant, standing within three inches of me, his head turned up to the sky that was clouding for snow, like he was trying to decide whether it would start to fall before or after dark and he didn't want to get caught in a storm on the road home.

What I can't figure out is how they missed him. The machine guns stopped and five NCO's rushed him at the same time from different ends of the range just as I got a good hold on his legs and pulled him down, expecting to get an armful of blood.

As they dragged him off, each one asking him why he did it, he muttered something about not believing they'd really use live bullets after the time his brother got killed. Well, as it turned out, they may as well have been blanks.

. . . From yours and everybody else's letters lately everything seems to be okay in Logan. Any work going on to speak of?

My buddy Rooks is in the violent ward of the hospital. I've never known a spark of violence out of him myself, but the army seems to like it that way.

. . . Well, I guess Rooks being gone did it, and maybe the way Rankin reacted to the gas drill.

For once, Rankin didn't listen to instructions, and when he went in this concrete shack and Sergeant Allen told him to take off his mask, he looked at the purple stuff puffing up out of that can on the floor and he panicked. Allen had to jerk it off of him, and then he struggled, and coughed, and Allen had to drag him out in the air.

I was next and I did what he told me. You're supposed to take the mask off and sniff the gas so you'll learn to recognize the odor, and then put the mask back on.

Tonight he called Rankin in his room and then he called me in and told me he was giving me a dry run on being squad leader.

. . . I was in charge of decorating the messhall for Thanksgiving Dinner and the colonel just happened to pick our company to bring his family to, and his wife said she felt right at home. I thought the place looked pretty good, but I don't think much of her idea of home.

. . . Allen took me with him to Columbia on a weekend pass and I had dinner with him and his wife, Peggy, and little boy, Rick. It was nice.

I went to see Rooks in the psycho ward at noon today and we played Chinese checkers.

. . . One of the guys I rode up with on the Greyhound bus went berserk this morning.

He's in a company up the street from us. He asked his company commander for permission to go home and be with his wife who was having a baby last night, and the CO told him he was a poor soldier and couldn't afford to miss the obstacle course today. This morning we were shivering in chow line when we heard a shot and PFC Faw (he got busted) said, "Some bolo done lost a toe."

Allen sat down at the squad leader's table and told us. This fellow got word his wife died in childbirth and the baby lived an hour, so he went right over to the CO's office, rendered the proper hand salute and shot him in the face.

. . . Dear Rachel, for some reason my orders didn't come through so I'm stuck here at the company for a few weeks and they've made me a regular cadre, working with the new cycle coming in on the bus next week. No furlough for me yet.

Goddamn it.

Frank leaned against the rangewall of the pit and lit a Robert Burns cigarillo.

"Hey, Frank!"

Frank made a roll turn along the wall and rested his arms on top of the sandbags. Among the gouges in the earth, he saw no one. The round dome of a helmet liner, one he had painted himself several months ago, rose up out of a hole in the ground, and then came Faw's eyes and his grin just before he sprung up from what was probably a kneeling position. Faw stood knee-deep where several grenades had burst. He saluted and fell backward, and all the soldiers in the new training cycle who were sitting under the linden trees, the branches swaying in the stout wind, the ice cracking after the morning rain, laughed.

The lieutenant in the tower didn't like any form of horseplay anywhere, especially not on the grenade range, so he reached for the mike. "PFC Faw, stop that clowning around down there."

Faw got up and walked toward the pits, stumbling intentionally in the holes. When he got to the pit where Frank leaned, watching him, he stepped off as if onto solid ground and when he started dropping, shot up his arm and pinched his nose. Lieutenant Grigger looked up at the sky, then started coughing and blowing into the mike to overcome the impulse to laugh.

Crouching behind him, grasping him under the armpits, Frank tried to help Faw up, until he realized Faw was playing rag doll and dropped him, too tired to contribute any physical exertion to Faw's compulsive horseplay. But when Faw, still holding his nose, tried to paddle to the surface of a deep pool, Frank could hardly get his breath for laughing.

In the two months Frank had known him, Faw clowned his way down a ladder of chevrons on his sleeve. It started, Allen told Frank, the first day under fire in Vietnam. Faw got hysterical and couldn't stop laughing, and when they told him about it later, he latched onto it as a gimmick of survival.

When he stood up, his face was straight. "Frank, you collect rare rocks?"

"Yeah," Frank said, going along with it.

"Here," Faw flipped up Frank's breast pocket, crammed a piece of shrapnel in it, and with a swipe of his thumb pressed the flap down again. "Merry Christmas, one week early."

"On your feet!" Lieutenant Grigger in the tower yelled over the PA system.

Faw did a Groucho dip-walk around the wall of sandbags that divided the pits.

Frank ground his cigarillo into the loose sand and dirt. He relaxed for the last round. The routine, the rhythm soothed him: the voice in the tower, monotonous but cadenced, the men stepping up from the waiting position, going through the five motions, each lineup ending in a swift series of explosions that made the ground tremble beneath Frank's feet and in his shoulder where he pressed up against the bags, head bowed. An easy, good way to kill time another day while waiting for the reassignment orders from personnel that the major promised would definitely be coming down.

He watched the men quick-time it toward the waiting line and the platoons that had already gone through scramble for the trucks where only four of them would be able to sit in the warm cab with the driver.

"Hustle! Hustle!" At the sound of Lieutenant Grigger's low, bored voice, the stragglers approaching the pit did a hop-skip and quickened their pace.

Frank watched Allen walk slowly toward the trucks and knew by his gait what he was going to do. The troops didn't know better, yet. "Fall out!"

Trying to get over the side of the truck bed, some did, knowing that the last one would ride the range.

"All right, men, you heard *and* saw the demonstrators," said Lieutenant Grigger. "You should know exactly what to do. But if I really thought you did, I'd . . ." He turned his head from the mike and Frank faintly heard him say to the NCO up in the tower with him, "Ringler, what's that truck up to?"

Frank walked up the slight incline out of the pit and saw a truck coming toward the training area out of the curving line of pine trees. It stopped beside the other trucks, behind the platoon Allen had called to attention. A trainee got out, wearing shiny new baggy fatigues, the nameplate blank, and Frank went back down into the pit and waited.

"Who is that man, Sergeant?"

Sergeant Mixon yelled up to the tower, "Regimental sent him over, sir. They want him to qualify with this company."

"All right, Sergeant, fill up one of those lines with him . . . . Now, men, listen to me," Lieutenant Grigger said, standing tall. "Every syllable. You are *on* the grenade range."

"Who dropped a rose?" said Faw, through a quarter-sized gap in the sandbag wall that partitioned the pits.

"If you don't know that by now, you shouldn't be here. And if I were one of the cadre *on* the ground, I know damn well I wouldn't *want* you here." After one man in the first round had laughed, not knowing that Lieutenant Grigger used that line almost every round and that it was no longer funny to him, nobody laughed. "You see *before* you ten pits. *In* each pit is a cadre, *holding* a live grenade. You are one man in a line of ten other men. You have been told what line to stand *in*. Are you standing in it? Are you standing *in* it?"

"Yes, sir!" They all sounded off.

"I wants to bless you," he said, grimly imitating Sergeant Ringler, who sat on the wooden railing of the tower, his helmet liner resting on the broken ridge of his nose, his boots resting on the bottom slat. When Frank was a trainee, Ringler bitched his group through the grenade range in a stiff wind, and the tower keeled over and he sprained his wrist. Now every chance he got, he was up in the tower, balanced on the rail.

"First line *enter* the pits!" Lieutenant Grigger suddenly shouted, slapping the railing. "Hustle! Hustle! The rest of you honchos stay, stay back *of* that wire. Sit!" Frank heard them shoosh to the ground, cartridge belts clinking. "You men *in* the pits. Take a good look *at* your cadre. He's real, made of flesh and blood, not a dummy put there to scare *you*. He wants to go on living even if you don't, so— McDaniel!"

"Yes, sir?"

"Where's *your* man?"

Frank looked around. "I don't know, sir."

"Young soldier," whispered Faw, through the little hole in the wall, "you'd better shape up."

"Sergeant Mixon!"

"He's coming, sir. Went to stack his rifle." Frank kicked gently at the sanded incline and looked at the rise where the helmeted heads moved behind the bank under the wire. A head rose up above the wire and a leg cocked to step over and it was Rooks.

Frank wanted to yell to the lieutenant that this man was from the psycho ward, but as Rooks loped down to the pit, Frank realized that they must have cleared him for return to training, right where he left off, skipping a rerun of the machine-gun range probably. The day after he went to the hospital, the company went on the grenade range, full of cute remarks about the kid who thought he was too good to crawl on his belly. Stumbling into the pit, he didn't even grin at Frank. Frank looked him full in the face for some sign, guarantee of sanity, but Rooks's eyes didn't register him.

"Hi, Rooks," Frank said.

"Hi," said Rooks, blinking his eyes. The voice from the tower startled Rooks, and he turned and shaded his eyes, looking up, grinning, as though the sun that hadn't shined all day were too bright.

"I'm going to go over it once more, men. On the count of one, you will, as a body, as a *body*, take into your right hand the grenade which the cadre on your right will hand you. If you are *left*-handed," he said, in the same tone he used on a boy who asked in the first round, "you will simply execute the marvelous maneuver of shifting it to your left hand. On the count of two, you will hook your index finger in the pinring, in the *pinring*. On the count of three, on the count of *three*, you will pull the pin out. On the count of four, you will cock your hand back, and in your head you will count three. On the count of five, on the count of five, I said on the count of *five*, you will throw that grenade as far as you possibly can, and then, without any encouragement from arithmetic, you will crouch down behind the barrier. The sound you hear will be that of a live, a *live* grenade, exploding as a result of your having pulled the pin."

"When in doubt," said Faw, "bug out," and Rooks didn't even turn to see who spoke through the gap in the sandbag wall between the pits.

Frank wondered what had gotten into Lieutenant Grigger, who usually allowed no embroidery of instructions, even on the dry run. It must have been Faw's clowning. It had finally gotten to him. And Sergeant Ringler's "I wants to bless you" had reached his manager-of-a-dry-goods-store soul.

Rooks hadn't taken his eyes off Lieutenant Grigger, or his hand from its shading position. Frank tensed.

"One more item. If, I say *if*, and goddam it, I mean *if*, one of you panics, I mean you got the pin out and it suddenly dawns on you that you've set loose what can blow your arm off, and you panic, and you can't throw, drop it, drop it, and let the cadre pick it up. Not *you*. *You* stay perfectly rigid, and let the cadre pick it up. Two heads, four arms, four feet, and a live grenade on the floor of a four-by-four pit is a mistake. So remember. You've pulled the pin, you can't throw, so you drop it."

"Come Saturday, short-timer," said Faw, through the hole, "let's me and you get drunk as two waltzing pissants."

"Now. Ready on the right? Ready on the left! Ready on the firing *line*! One!"

Frank handed Rooks the grenade.

"Two!"

Rooks hooked his finger in the pinring, and on the nail there was still some green polish a whore in Columbia had painted on his fingernails and toenails while he slept.

"Three!"

Rooks pulled the pin.

"Four!"

Rooks dropped the grenade and went rigid.

"Goddamn you!" Frank dropped to his knees and reached for the grenade as it rolled down the slight incline.

"Five!"

"I'm sorry, he said, 'Drop it on four.'" Rooks fell to his knees opposite Frank, the grenade rolled into his cupped hands, and he smiled. Frank rose and slid, trying to get up the loose incline.

All the grenades exploded.

Looking at the Dead

For some people, Jefferson Highway starts somewhere in Canada. A marker tells where it ends at St. Charles Street in New Orleans. For other people, Jefferson Highway starts at the marker on St. Charles Street in New Orleans and ends somewhere in Canada. I don't know. I was never there.

Jefferson Highway passes through Baton Rouge, Louisiana, at seven o'clock Sunday morning, August 17, 1983. Sunlight moving in the spanish moss of live oaks soothes the driver of a car (who started neither somewhere in Canada nor at St. Charles Street, nor will he end at either place), makes him go slow. As the driver feels the glide into a curve, not seeing his aerial flick a low-hanging drape of moss, a horse runs, panic in its eyes, toward the hood. The driver doesn't know that the concrete hurts its unshod hoofs. He sees that its hide is tan, its mane and tail blond, it goes from dark brown to light brown, and sunlight dapples it when it can. Galloping straight at the hood, it will not leap, soar, over the car.

No rain falls, the mist has dissolved. Sunlight and running horse, running swiftly but seeming to gallop slow-motion because the driver has never seen a loose horse. It is freedom running, a pure event of the morning—that's what he sees on this short stretch that he is traveling between Canada and New Orleans. And each instant, the horse makes this stretch shrink, into itself, *himself*, the driver now sees.

This driver is no more captive than most men. He does not project onto the running horse his own idea of freedom. He beholds freedom as a pure act of running. Though he is free to turn off this highway and take alternate routes, even to turn back, change course, he does not feel in the engine the freedom he sees in the horse. He has felt before on lonely, late-night highways a oneness of his own metabolism with the minute explosions of the engine, and freedom was what he called that feeling, but what he sees running past him, now sees looking back over his shoulder, slowing down the car, then sees in the rearview mirror as he goes on, light-footed on the accelerator, is *turned-looseness*. Having jumped a fence. Having pushed through a gap in a gate. Having seen a hole in a fence not there before. The driver's last glimpse of the horse: he turns in at a driveway, leaping over the morning paper.

Loving freedom, though not horses particularly, but saddened by the image of a horse smashed by a surprised car or truck, the driver looks for a likely house, a fenced-in place, other horses standing around under a tree. A mile ahead, he sees horses in the shade of many trees, but not the sagging barbed wire, or the concrete pullover, from which a broad drive slopes to a sprawling Spanish-style house.

We have seen the driver and the horse see and pass each other on Jefferson Highway, and we know the driver's heart beat fast because freedom ran toward him, then beat faster because when the horse passed, he imagined a violent collision. For us, this man's moment has passed. We will never see him again. Nor the horse.

If the world is all one breathing, can I imagine with a guiltless innocence that a family lies dead in that house? Does what I imagine have no consequence? Do only physical acts reverberate throughout creation?

You may or may not choose to return to the concrete pullover and descend the slope to the Spanish ranch-style house. But I have made *my* choice. In this paragraph I begin as a murderer.

Somebody else who is alive is already in the house. I am afraid that if I give him a name and history, he will become real, and I do not want him to suffer what he sees. I do know that two years from now, on November 3, 1985, at 3 PM, at the intersection of Fairmount and Market in San Diego, he will run down the man who drove past this house a few moments ago, he will drive on in panic, and the face of the man will haunt him the rest of his life, for he is not a killer. But that will happen in the real world; I am not responsible.

I do not mean to imply that he does not suffer as I imagine him walking through this house. But I refuse to describe his feelings.

This man, maybe he is old, maybe he is young, maybe he is white, maybe he is black, perhaps he limps, entered the house to commit a burglary. I will say this much about his feelings as he entered the house through the back door (one of hundreds he has entered): the instant his foot touched the kitchen floor, bliss. He enters to enter. But once inside, he feels a compulsion to justify, on a practical plane, the act of entry. He has a compulsion to gaze upon people who are sleeping, and in their presence take something that belongs to them.

He has looked upon everything in the house now, upon each person in the family and upon all the objects in the rooms, and now I am waiting for him to come out. I don't want him in the house when we enter.

We do not enter through the back door as the burglar did. We are simply there, suddenly, in the dining room. And now we no longer speak of you and me.

For twelve hours, no heat has risen from the steak bones, water does not swell the cells of the lettuce in the salad bowls.

In his den, T. K. does not read in a two-day-old edition of the *State-Times*: "This capital, wrapped up in the world's problems, discovered Thursday it has a little boy so lonely he ran with packs of dogs at night for companionship." He does not think, I would like to adopt that little fellow.

Where chair legs and eight shod, two bare, feet pressed it down, the nap of the pale green rug does not rise.

The hinges of her jaws, the muscles of her cheeks do not open Judith's mouth.

In Barbara's ears, there is no sound of a match being struck then spewing into flame, no smoke enters her lungs.

Sabra does not remove the long black false eyelashes she bought to wear on stage as Blanche du Bois.

The toilet in Ramsay's bathroom does not flush.

Spittle in T. K.'s pipe does not dribble on his chin.

The shower does not gush scalding hot, then lukewarm.

Barbara's hand does not smooth the pages of *McCall's*.

The sun does not shine through the trees, casting shadows over the walls of Judith's room, the curtains, brushed by her naked body when she passed, do not shudder.

Sabra does not read the headline on the back page of the *State-Times*: "Highway Patrolman Quits / 'I Don't Mind the Dead . . . It's Watching Them Die.'"

The prints of Ramsay's feet coming in from the pool are not wet.

On Sabra's lightly roughed cheeks, her mascaraed eyelids, tears do not glisten.

Barbara's panties are not warm with the scent of her delicate discharge.

T. K. does not listen for his private phone in his impaneled den to ring.

The warmth of bodies is no longer fixed in the fibres of the woven cane of the five chairs pushed back from the table, and the sixth chair, shoved up to the table, is cold.

Judith does not kiss her reflection in the mirror on her bedroom wall, or laugh and think of herself as a fool.

Molecules of earwax and chlorinated water do not smell fresh in Ramsay's nostrils.

The pink towel does not remain tightly wadded.

Sabra does not pray to Jesus that her sister Barbara is not pregnant.

The mirror in Barbara's room does not reflect her naked body in profile, the slightly rounded belly, the blond fuzz golden against the light coming through a slit in the red curtains.

T. K. does not pick up his private phone, dial a number, then immediately hang up.

The singing in the oaks outside her window does not make Judith wish she were a bird, and the whinnying of the horses does not make her want to ride to the Mississippi in the moonlight naked.

The green salamander does not cross the screen, silvered by the light of dusk, stop, and blow up its pale red sack.

Ramsay's thumb print on the edge of the Joplin LP is not moist, in the back of his stereo, the tubes, which he still has not seen, are not hot.

The ink from Barbara's pen is not wet on the letter folded inside the violet envelope, addressed to Doug on Parris Island.

The pages of RABBIT IS RICH do not make a sibilant sound every forty seconds fifty times between Judith's fingers.

On the paneled wall, the glassy eyes of the stuffed zebra do not reflect a distorted image of the garden door across the room opening, admitting moonlight, then Barbara in her gown, and T. K.'s eyes do not open at the sound of the doorknob turned loose.

The images conjured up by CANDY do not give Ramsay an erection.

The muscles of stomachs have ceased to grind the food that, cut from stuff still on the plates, left the table, and small intestines have ceased to secrete digestive juices.

Sabra's ankle does not itch, the mosquito bite has stopped swelling, the poison is not virulent.

The television in Barbara's room is not off.

T. K.'s semen does not spurt into Judith's vagina and mingle with the secretions from her own glands that he once said smelled as sweet as gun oil.

The pungent odor from the open whiskey bottle hidden under Ramsay's bed has not stopped filling the air.

The blue horsefly does not circle T. K.'s leather lounge in his den, his moustache does not twitch in sleep.

For six hours, the smell of horses has not been strong on Judith's hands.

T. K. does not hear a gun go off behind him, turn and fail to hear the second blast.

Barbara does not hear shots, think it is a car backfiring up on

Jefferson Highway, then moments later realize she had heard shots in the house.

A bullet does not shatter Judith's brain.

Ramsay is not awakened by a scream.

Blood does not spurt out of Barbara's neck.

The hairs on Ramsay's chest do not mat the blood from his heart.

Lungs do not inhale oxygen, exhale carbon dioxide.

The telephone does not ring the first time since dinner.

Feet, carrying bodies from room to room, do not feel the solid floors.

The telephone does not ring the second time since dinner.

Pictures and paintings are not taken for granted.

The telephone does not ring the third time since dinner.

Flesh does not emit auras, minute flares of energy.

Tongues do not lick lips.

The telephone does not ring the fourth time since dinner.

Buttocks do not crush the fabrics of clothes, or leather, or cotton, or silk sheets.

Flowers are not received by eyes and nostrils as flowers.

In the moonlight that comes through the windows, glinting off the water faucets above the zinc sink, semen gleams, cools on the lime plate on the kitchen table.

Roaches do not stop gnawing on the teeth-scraped artichoke leaves.

Vomit on the living room rug is cooling.

The telephone rings for the first time since the burglar left the house.

The living are captive now in the house.